P9-CNB-600

F
TALLENT

Tallent, Elizabeth,
1954-

Honey.

DATE			

BAKER & TAYLOR BOOKS

HONEY

HONEY

stories

Elizabeth Tallent

ALFRED A. KNOPF

New York   1993

Some of the stories in this volume originally appeared in somewhat different
form in the following publications: *Grand Street*: "Ciudad Juárez" and
"Honey"; *Lear's*: "Get It Back for Me"; *Los Angeles Times Magazine*: "James
Was Here"; *The New Yorker* and *Best American Short Stories of 1990*: "Prowler";
Ploughshares: "Kid Gentle"; *The Taos Review*: "Earth to Molly" (originally titled
"Wing"); and *Zyzzyva*: "Black Dress."

Library of Congress Cataloging-in-Publication Data
Tallent, Elizabeth, [date]
Honey : stories / by Elizabeth Tallent. — 1st ed.
p.   cm.
ISBN 0-394-58304-3
1. Marriage—United States—Fiction.   I. Title.
PS3570.A398H65   1993
813'.54—dc20   93-18235
                                                          CIP

For Gabriel

If only I could concentrate on my plans,
If only I could keep my mind on the aims in my heart.

—improvised Hopi song,
quoted by Peter Whiteley in *Bacavi*

Contents

HONEY

Prowler

A new development, and more than he can bear: his ex-wife is suddenly back from Europe, her boyfriend of the last two years nowhere in sight. The tortoiseshell glasses she has never worn before alert him that Christie, confronting him across his own living room, has reinvented herself yet again. That the glasses still excite her as a novelty, a kind of prop, is plain to Dennis only because he knows her so well. She has a new gesture, index finger laid against the bridge of her nose to give the specs a tiny upward shove, brown eyes widening, that manages to get across the impression she is taking life more seriously, yet her account of the last year smells of evasiveness. Déjà vu, because his own sense, with Christie, was often that she was skipping details that might not reflect well on her, editing and enlarging as she went, and that he was essentially helpless to pin her to the truth. Christie is all in baggy black, her legs crossed, one black, doltish boot swinging. She wants their son for the summer.

"George has stayed behind," she says with a faint, enigmatic tone of apology. Not even that is clear. Not "I've left him" or "It was all a mistake," but "George has stayed behind." In Paris, where she lived with him for the last year.

By a coincidence, he and Christie both began second families last year, she with George, Dennis with his young wife Francesca. Christie's baby girl has been left in Santa Fe with a sitter. His twins are asleep upstairs with their mother, all of them exhausted by the cold they have been sharing back and forth. Andy, his and Christie's thirteen-year-old, is away overnight with his best friend; when Dennis heard a car grind to a halt in the rocky drive, he had a scared flash that Andy and Leo had got into trouble and somebody had been sent to tell him so. For next to no reason, Dennis distrusts Leo, a smart, good-looking kid, self-assured around adults in a way Andy never will be, not until he's one himself—maybe not even then. Leo's girlfriend works in a record store where Andy and Leo are always hanging out. Andy can't drive yet, of course, and neither can Leo. It's real proof of Leo's fast-talking charm that he has a sixteen-year-old girlfriend. Leo's mother, who doesn't approve of the girlfriend, drives the boys to the mall, because otherwise, she says, they'd hitchhike. Maybe it's Leo's mother Dennis dislikes. She gives in to the boys too easily. She was Christie's lawyer, trim and venomous, during the divorce.

What kind of trouble does he imagine his son getting into? Dennis has no very persistent or obsessive idea, just occasional glints in which Andy pockets a Baggie of white powder or, with faked knowingness, hoovers a furled five-dollar bill over a mirror, talked into these idiot risks by Leo. None of those fears come true; instead an altogether different problem materializes. The car that startled him belongs to Andy's mother.

Christie's never been in this house before, and one of his reactions to letting her in strikes Dennis as inappropriate, even disturbingly so, and he hides it: he'd like to know what she thinks. An architect, he is constantly exposed in his work to the wanton quest for the famous New Mexico light, which is especially sought after by new arrivals from the grayed-over, greenhoused cities of the East Coast. It's as if light is another aspect of the West they can seize and display, the way their walls are now hung with pristine longhorn and bison skulls whose flesh—the new arrivals don't trouble to learn this—has been boiled from the bone in oil drums, not worried away by coyotes. Dead Tech, Dennis's partner calls it. When Dennis first came across this house, it was a warren of low-ceilinged rooms whose windows were unfashionably small and few. Huge cottonwoods grew right up to the walls. Such a shaded, wood-fragrant, down-at-heels little place; he wanted it. In renovating, he changed it only minimally.

"Nice," Christie says of the room, sitting, crossing her black legs, beginning to pick at the cuticle of her thumb, and he asks himself why he wanted more of her. Glancing up, she reads his disappointment, and makes a face. *What do you expect?* the face says. This is where you live your new life. The face implies that she knew such a muted reaction would hurt. More than anything, he wants her to stop picking away at her cuticle. If she can get at him so fast, so nonchalantly, he'd better watch it.

"Can we turn on another light?" she asks.

When he does, he has to admire the kinked mass of her dark hair, backlit. Even with the stupid glasses, she looks good. She's already lost whatever weight she gained with the baby.

"Coffee?" he says, for a chance to leave the room. He pokes through a drawer for filters, then stares around the kitchen, catching his emotional breath, reorienting himself. "Tea," Christie calls. Her tone's not rude, and he's no longer annoyed with her, but it troubles him that, this long divorced, it's taken them all of five minutes to fall back into marital shorthand. O.K. Tea. By the time he carries their two cups back with him, he's both more guarded and surer about where to begin.

"Christie, weeks went by when you didn't call him. Once you let it go a month. February, right?"

She has too much at stake to lose her temper. That would have been her familiar next move, but she holds it fast, though her black thug's boot kicks air. "It costs a fortune."

"Do you think he understood being abandoned for a year? Then you show up here and you'd like to pick up right"— Dennis snaps his fingers—"where you left off."

"Did he tell you he felt abandoned by me? Are those his words?"

"The agreement that you get him summers depended on your trustworthiness."

"You're saying I have to be as predictable as you are, Dennis. You're saying I should never have had George in my life. I don't think that was the agreement."

A sort of ongoing record of their exchange—the conversation as he will replay it for Francesca—runs through his mind. Francesca, as she will sit up in their bed, listening, taking everything in, sometimes shaking her head or marveling aloud, is his sanity. Francesca illustrates children's books. Christie's mercurial excess, which prevents her carrying anything through to the end, and Francesca's serene attention to detail—to root, trunk, twig, and every small, slanting leaf in the forest—could not be further apart.

What fairy tale is it, where someone comes back at last for the beloved child? Because she's never seen well in the dark he walks Christie out to her car. When a rock trips her, he catches her arm, and in the darkness she twists to face him before shaking off his hand. She would rather have fallen. They could be any bitter couple walking in the woods, tired of each other, tired of the way nothing is ever resolved between them. He had thought he was protected from such vivid involuntary remembrance of her past lives: her zazen phase, with its hours of formidable silence; the year during which she was convinced she was an actress; the macrobiotic diet she starved herself on; the novel she finished half of. Leaving her had been so plainly necessary that he should not find himself surprised to be here, where everything, the house behind them, the wife sleeping soundly in that house, even the trees closing in around them, speaks of the care with which he has constructed an existence of his own. There is an infant's car seat in the back of her Volvo, and she has wedged a bag of groceries into it, upright. So this visit really was on the spur of the moment.

Leaning into her window as she starts the Volvo, wanting to end on a friendlier note, he asks whether she's found a place to live. She did. A week ago. In one of those apartment complexes where there's always something empty; he knows it.

But then she can't resist circling back to their quarrel. "So you're saying no for the summer?"

"Too much has changed for that agreement to hold."

"What's changed is that you're even more judgmental than before."

"You hurt him," he says.

"Dennis, we need to talk about this again." She takes a

hand from the wheel, raking her hair from her face, the dark-rimmed glasses picking up spots of light from somewhere. "I'll call," she says, and he can't tell her not to.

Tonk, plunk: something goes in upstream, where half-submerged boulders catch direct moonlight. All around Dennis, cottonwoods yield to the wind with saddling-up creaks. By the moonlight he observes them, the only trees he will ever think of as his own. A head black and broad as a Labrador's, and as purposefully at home, shaves across the glassy, swelling smoothness that is the deepest part of the river. A beaver, a big one, and upwind, or it would have known Dennis was there. *Castrados,* the beavers are called in Spanish, because after a fight the victorious male scythes off the scrotum of the loser, or so it's said. Dennis finds it hard to believe, but since hearing it he likes the beavers less than he did before, when he thought they mutilated only his ancient cottonwoods. Another bit of folklore: the piss of a man connotes a proprietary interest that the beavers tend to respect. Each night Dennis liberates a different tree from possible destruction. Barefoot, brooding, he smells the odor his urine gives to dry, grateful old bark, and taps the last drops onto a golden leaf. The spring wind, balmy and humid, blows across the river, and as it stirs Dennis's hair there is that slight, single instant in which he feels himself blameless.

His divorce seems a tight black tunnel he once forced himself and Andy through, fearing each forward move, fearing still more getting stuck to suffocate. A blindly crawling exit from pain, his shy kid shoved along before him. So Andy loves motorcycles, which do not creep, which proclaim in every line speed and certainty. Christie didn't ask, or didn't think she could ask, to see Andy's room. Dennis believes it tells everything about Andy. Photo-realist motorcycles, chrome and highly evolved threat, grace the walls, along with a passport photo of Kafka razor-bladed from a library biography, a sin so small and inexplicable, and finally so appealing, that Dennis uncharacteristically forgot to mention it to Andy. If Andy's motorcycle paintings, done in this hyper attentive style of glisten and mass, are depressing, surely jug-eared Kafka promises complexity, contradiction, hope? When he was a little boy, Andy painted houses with peaked roofs, surreal cats and dogs and birds, petroglyph parents—Dennis and Christie— with their hands linked over the head of a smaller, round-eyed creature, Andy himself. Orange sun, blue house, green grass, all's well. The garish houses dwindled; cats and dogs were supplanted by snakes and wolves; Dennis and Christie were replaced by superbly muscled superheroes, and Andy was seven. Ten was the year of the divorce. Thirteen is this plague of motorcycles, Leo's flawless smile, and hanging out at the mall. Oddly—at least Dennis wouldn't have predicted it— Andy wrote regularly to his mother in France. Because Andy didn't seem to consider them particularly private, Dennis sometimes read the letters over Andy's shoulder. The light of the computer screen glowed on his son's clear forehead. He wanted her to know that he liked having a little sister. He wanted her to know that he thought about her. He really worked on the letters. None of the obvious things (When was she coming home? Ever?) were in the letters. His son knew by thirteen not to ask Christie certain questions.

At the kitchen table Dennis eats slices of bologna folded into cold tortillas and drinks a beer, then scrapes and washes the day's dishes while the twins' bottles come bobblingly to a boil on the back of the stove. When Gavin wails, Dennis climbs the cantilevered stairs. Tim howls, coming to consciousness alongside his brother. Dennis lights a candle, his habit so that the overhead light won't blind Francesca, blinking awake. Dennis lays Gavin and Tim side by side on the bed, and Francesca sits up. Theirs is a four-handed assembly line, the twins' bottoms bared, wiped, and rediapered, neither boy crying, both staring from their giant calm father to their giant calm mother, who are talking softly together. Francesca takes Gavin. He can't lunge at the breast fast enough, and she laughs down at him. Though they're almost over the cold, the twins' breathing remains raspy. The wings of Francesca's nose are coarsely red, and her chest has the tonic stink of Vicks Vapo-Rub, which neither boy seems to mind. Dennis cradles Tim, leaning back in an old chair whose upholstery is a kind of friendly maroon moss worn away, on the arms, in matching bald spots his elbows fit in as he angles the bottle up. Tim's warm head rests in a hand large enough to cup it completely. What weight was ever this good? A baseball fresh from the sporting-goods store, or his high-school girlfriend's breasts released from lacy bra cups in a dark Chevrolet. Maybe. Francesca is uneasy, Dennis can tell. She's not sure she understands exactly what is wrong, though he's told her everything that was said.

He says, "She can't have him this summer."

"Andy has a father *and* a mother."

That lightly stressed *"and"* is criticism, and subtle as it is, it pricks him to argue, "You wouldn't know that by the last year."

"She was far away."

"That's no excuse," he says, knowing she knows it's not, having advanced it only so that they could both examine its weakness—could study, through the excuse's transparency, Christie's habitual irresponsibility. For a time they sit quietly, each with an urgently sucking baby, until, in Dennis's arm, Tim yawns, a thumb gliding into his mouth, his body's weight going sated and more vague, so that it's only a matter of settling him into the crib. Then Dennis leans to take Gavin. This is tense: Gavin's crying, if it starts, will rouse his brother, but Gavin sleeps. Ah, silence. "We're good," Dennis says, and the answer is an amused "Good? Great." He sits on the bed, not ready yet to climb under the covers, some chord in him still vibrating at a tense, post-Christie pitch. Francesca stretches, then narrows her attention until it includes only him. To do this, she very deliberately excludes sleep. The intense, the velvety deep desirability of unbroken sleep is what Dennis senses most strongly whenever he enters this room. In any competition he wages for her against sleep, sleep's going to win. It has only to lap inward from the dim corners of the room to close over her head, and she has only to let herself slide luxuriously under, while what he wants, in wanting to make love, would ask effort of her, and an energy she doesn't have.

"Showing up here with no warning," Francesca says.

"It was weird."

"No wonder you resent it, but what convinced you she can't have Andy?"

"She's lost the boyfriend."

Francesca says, "What has that got to do with it, really?"

"How many guys does Andy get to see come and go?"

"In three years there's been George. Not exactly promiscuous."

"Now Andy has a sister he knows only from pictures."

"The sister was born in Paris," she says reasonably. "Andy can get to know her here."

He wants Francesca on his side, not mediating between him and Christie. "She kept talking in non sequiturs." He places his hands, palms facing, in the air before her, implying the gaps between what Christie said and what she said next, but Francesca leans forward until his hands slide into a caress of her face, until, with two fingers, he tucks hair behind an ear, and then idly revolves the pearl resting against that ear's lobe, as if he were turning a tiny screw, tightening some connection that had, minutely, loosened.

"What's her baby's name?"

"Emma." He feels strange, saying it.

"I'd hate to see you be so unforgiving toward me," she says.

After a time he tells her thoughtfully, "I couldn't be," but she's asleep, her mouth open, an arm flung out before her, her fingers touching the wall, her entire body relaxed, loose, her fingertips' pressure against the wall too negligible, too accidental, to suggest she is meeting any resistance, even in a dream.

The next afternoon Andy comes in, home from somewhere, on his way somewhere else, and is struck enough by his father's expression to say, "You look weird." Dennis, lying back on his son's unmade bed under the portrait of a glitteringly malign Harley-Davidson, squeezing a racquetball in his left hand, answers, "Your mom's back."

Two squeezes of the ball before Andy risks "Yeah?" He is careful not to let slip how pleased he is, but in a lilting involuntary movement, younger than he is, he goes up on his toes, his long legs braced, and bounces, one arm holding the other arm at the elbow.

Dennis says, "Uh-huh. Just last week. She came over last night."

"She did? Is that what's wrong with you?"

"What's wrong with me is no sleep and I didn't shave and that makes me feel old." He dents the blue racquetball with his thumb, and it oozes back into its sphere as he remembers that when his own father used to say he felt old it was a threat that Dennis suffered with an obscure and embarrassed guilt.

He reads in his son the same stiffening, the same resentment, as Andy, at his dresser, fidgets a drawer open and shut, and Dennis says to his back, appealing to the cocky set of the shoulders and the vulnerability of the nape exposed by the cruel Leo-like haircut, "Look, I wanted you to know, but I was really thinking you could spend the summer here. With us."

"You hate her," Andy says intensely, talking down into the drawer, and Dennis starts to say "No, Andy, that's not it" when Andy strips off his sweatshirt, tearing it over his head, its shapely unknowable stubbornness so much like his mother's, and Dennis sees the violent bruise marbling his son's arm. The bruise resolves into a tattoo of a skeleton on a motorcycle, leaning forward as if into wind, black eye sockets, spiked helmet, the whole evil deal, grinning on the freckled, pale, still baby-fattish curve of adolescent biceps. Dennis slams the racquetball at the wall. It caroms past Andy's shoulder. "Dad!" Andy cries, and Dennis is up, taking two fast steps, grabbing the arm. Andy twists away to stand against the wall, cornered.

"My God, it's ugly." Dennis hears the hoarseness of his own voice, the sound of a father's barely controlled anger. "I didn't want to believe it was real. Was this Leo's idea?"

"No. Mine. Dad, it didn't hurt. The needles were really clean. I watched the guy sterilize them. That's the first thing you see when you walk into his place, this big sterilizer. Dad, it's my body. You would have said no. You know you would have said no."

It's my body. Dennis can't believe that. He can't conceive of having no say in what happens to this body, in no longer being needed to protect it. Andy is five, shuddering in his arms; he has fallen into a doorjamb, slitting open his lower lip, and for some reason Dennis is catching the blood in his hand. Andy is two, shrieking down at his own bare leg as the needle eases in. The nurse has told Dennis, who wanted to hold Andy in his lap, facing his chest, that it's better if Andy sees that it's the nurse who's hurting him. That way Andy won't come to distrust his own father.

"What does it mean?" Dennis asks.

"It doesn't mean anything. It's just cool."

"You're thirteen years old," Dennis says, "and you'll be living with this the rest of your life."

"I want to live with it." Andy pulls on a clean sweatshirt from his drawer, and the tattoo disappears under a sleeve. What Andy's defensive about, it hits Dennis, is that he does not regret the grinning little leather-jacketed Death on its motorcycle. Part of him would like to drum up regret if that's the clue to his father's forgiveness, but the truth is he's now too old to summon emotion on demand, and too honest to fake it, without being insulated enough to fight his father without a fair amount of pain. Dennis catches himself making an abrupt accommodating shift, with this insight, in the direction of understanding his son as someone strictly separate from him. Perhaps the tattoo has accomplished what it was meant to. Perhaps it was meant to be something that couldn't be undone and something he couldn't possibly like about his child. That's it. His adoration has been unconditional. He's made Andy have to wrestle it off. Something has changed between them, and here Andy is, watching him covertly for signs that this is over. Over, so that he can go.

"You were so perfect when you were born," Dennis says, and is blindsided by the idea that the only other person who will truly mourn that perfection as he does is Christie. "You're grounded," Dennis says. "You're not leaving this house."

When the phone rings that night, Francesca answers and mouths, "It's her." Dennis shakes his head. Holding Gavin against her shoulder, Francesca mouths, "Come on." He holds his left hand flat in the air, his right vertically below it, a T. Time out. Francesca, exasperated, has just enough grace to

smile at him. She says, "Christie, he must have gone out. I
didn't hear him leave. Andy?" Dennis is shaking his head
furiously. "Andy's out with Leo. Sorry. I'll tell them both you
called."

Two nights later, and this time Francesca's side of the
conversation is "He never called you? I gave him your message.
I am sorry. His partner's away, so, you know. I'm sure he'll
get back to you as soon as he can." Francesca listens a moment
before adding, "I *agree* with you this can't go on much longer."
When she hangs up, Francesca says, "Did you hear that last
part?"

"I need time," he says.

She shakes her head at his hard anger, at how far he's
willing to take this. "She's not helpless," Francesca says. "She
can always call her lawyer. I think you're in the wrong."

Without her on it, his side begins to strike him as stale,
small-minded, and increasingly indefensible, and a day later
it comes to him that it's time he talked to Christie. Francesca
seems relieved, looking up from a drawing of a wolf, forepaws
resting together on a green satin coverlet, one incisor exposed,
caught outside the lip in accidental malice, the whiskers long,
flexed back against the muzzle in a grimace of grandmotherly
welcome.

"Nice," Dennis says, and amends this to "Great. That wolf
has eaten people."

"Did you know your eyes are red?"

"It's insomnia, not your cold. Don't worry."

"How can anyone not sleep?" she says. "I love sleep."

They're both startled by a sneeze, followed by syrupy
coughs, from the bedroom overhead where the twins nap,
and Francesca says, "If they get sick again, I'm going to kill
myself."

He leaves his office early to go to Christie's apartment. It's
in a stucco complex of separate four-story buildings spaced

around culs-de-sac and traffic islands spiked with dying yucca.
He should have called her first, but somehow, for all his keyed-
up restlessness, he never got around to it. "You look terrible,"
people kept telling him all day, and he got tired of his own
small joke, "I feel much worse than I look." Well, she surprised
him, showing up without warning. Surely she can't be too put
off if he does the same. When his knocks go unanswered,
he scratches in the dirt under a flourishing white geranium.
Christie's houseplants always thrived. She always left a key
under one of her plants by the front door, though he'd asked
her not to a thousand times. He lets himself in, telling himself
he's going to call out to see if she's there after all, but once
inside he makes no sound. Stealth, it strikes him, is no small
thing, but very physical. He's breathing faster than he likes,
as if he'd run two miles on the river road, his heart banging.
Her baby's toys lie all around. The bright clutter, for some
reason, panics him. In his own house, he would begin picking
things up; he'd know how to go about setting things straight.
Here, he can't. He's stymied by the very fact that he's an
intruder. An intruder is an unreasonable thing to be. *You are
in the wrong,* maybe more deeply than ever before. Leo's mother
could make a capital case out of this. As if with foresight, he
dressed for the part. His Levi's are torn, and his shabby sneakers, gray with age, let him move neatly, brimming with guilt
and yet slightly high on it, through the mess, which seems to
him evidence of happiness, her happiness, which he long ago
divorced himself from, which he has no right to know anything
of. All this, everything he sees, is contraband. A jack-in-the-
box has been left as it was, sprung open, the vacantly grinning
head hanging upside down from the long caterpillarlike sleeve
of the body, and here is a naked doll seated in a chair, and on
the couch *Vanity Fair* open to a picture of Kevin Costner,
leaning back, his shirt loose, glass in hand. Dennis feels scath-
ingly appraised by Kevin Costner.

On the far side of a narrow counter is the kitchen, whose paint-splattered furniture she must have got at the Salvation Army. Four straight-backed chairs are dashed with brilliant blue, while the small table is a scarred palette of yellow, turquoise, hot pink, and silver. It looks as if an Abstract Expressionist went insane here. There are crumbs of burned toast in the high chair's tray. The floor is fifties linoleum, tan tiles with faint white cirrus clouds drifting across them, and on one tile, Christie—or someone—has painted a tiny airplane. She has been using *The Frugal Gourmet,* which is propped open by her mother's (he remembers) tin recipe box. In the refrigerator, nothing much—milk, bread, juice, the usual, and a half-empty bottle of Beaujolais with the cork floating in the wine. She never handled corkscrews well. Peanut butter. Garlic, fat cloves in mauve-white paper. He takes the garlic out—garlic doesn't belong in the refrigerator—but, holding the crisp little weight, he doesn't know what to do with it. If he leaves it out, she's going to know somebody was here. He has to put it back. He does.

Emma's room, sunny and disheveled, the crib against a wall on which hangs a small Amish quilt, its corners frayed, a powdery-pleasant baby smell and folded clothes in wire drawers under a changing table. A basket of teething rings. A kazoo. A child's rocker. Balled up in the crib, a pair of baby tights and a striped sock. A second small bedroom, darker, shades down, must be meant for Andy. There's something wonderful in being in this room, and he's still high on his amazed apprehension of his own wrongdoing, floating on it, willing to stay with it a little longer now that he's come this far. His hearing is sharp, but there's nothing, no sound, and his sense of what he's seeing seems magnificently, magically clear. He wouldn't have known any of this. She would never have told him. Even if she'd wanted to tell him, he wouldn't have listened. Here are things she thinks Andy will like: a cowboy bedspread, a glaring African mask, an aquarium filled with water, oxygen percolating through it, no fish yet but some kind of seaweed hypnotically weaving, and, clinging to the glass, snails small as capers. A desk fashioned from a sheet of Melamite laid over sawhorses. A bright-blue dresser. The drawers, when he opens them, are empty, except that the last drawer contains a Hershey's Kiss.

As he sits heavily on the bed, his exhilaration dies. It doesn't so much desert him in a rush as evaporate, and a befuddling gray fatigue fogs over the vacuum it leaves in him. This stupid midafternoon sleepiness feels entirely ordinary. He lies back on the bed and puts an arm over his face, breathing in the smell of himself—slightly sweaty, salty guilt. Still no sound. It feels good. He even feels he's in the right place.

He dreams a dream he thinks of later as intended for Andy. Andy should have dreamed it; by accidentally falling asleep in this bed, Dennis got it. In it, Christie is younger, Andy barely old enough to work a scissors, the two of them sitting on the floor with their dark heads together, cutting animals from construction paper, the air between them charged with great, disinterested tenderness, and they're not talking. The animals they cut out come alive. A monkey jumps to his knee, and Andy giggles. Christie sets a blue giraffe down on the floor and it canters stiffly away. Waking, Dennis's first thought is that he's dreamed a dream he wasn't in. He can't remember ever having had such a dream before. In some subtle shift in the room's shadows he reads a new degree of lateness, of sheer wrongness in being here, and his body responds with a rising thrill of adrenaline, but he still doesn't move. He wonders if what he really wants is to get caught. In another minute he's able to tell himself *That would really be the height of stupidity,* and he sits up. His body hates his refusal to get moving. He shakes his head to clear the last of the sleep from it, but the mysterious peacefulness of the dream still has a hold on him. What he's seen won't let go so easily.

Back through the apartment, each object in its place, everything exactly as he found it, it begins to appear to him that he's getting away with this. He lets himself out and finds that it's later than he thought, probably six-thirty or so. When he checks the parking lot two stories down, she's not there: her dark-rimmed glasses aren't aimed upward in accusation, and though he fumbles, locking the door, her Volvo does not materialize. He twitches geranium leaves out of the way, sliding the key back where she likes it.

This is not happiness, just a gaudy physiological response to not getting caught—light head, hands shaking, legs he has to will steady to get himself down the stairs, world that looks entirely strange.

"I thought I couldn't leave the house until I was thirty-two," Andy says, his feet on the dash, looking around the maze of stucco buildings he's never seen before.

"You can't," Dennis says. "The one place you can come is here. I want you to call me for your ride home. No taking off. No improvising."

"But I can stay the weekend."

"You can stay the weekend if you want."

"Why?"

"I was wrong before," Dennis says. "I was just wrong."

"But how did you see you were wrong?"

"You don't get to know all the details."

"Does Mom?"

"I haven't talked to her."

"You mean she doesn't know I'm coming?"

"She's home. There's her car, right?"

"I don't like surprising her," Andy says.

"O.K. You really don't like it, we turn around, we drive home, we get on the phone, we arrange this for some other time. Is that how you want to do this?"

He hesitates, and then says, "I guess so." Dennis starts the car; maybe this was a bad idea, but he'd liked the feel of it. He'd wanted to change things all at once. He'd wanted the suddenness of his reversal on his side in convincing Christie that things were going to be different from now on, and he hadn't guessed that it might be Andy who didn't like the idea, who seemed unprepared for it.

"Stop," Andy says, removing his feet from the dash, sitting up. "I'm going, O.K.?"

"Whatever you want to do."

"I'll call you."

"Call."

He's gone. He's on the stairs, bag on his shoulder, lighter-footed than his father can remember ever being, taking the two flights of stairs as if they are nothing. Then Christie is at the door in black jeans, a man's T-shirt huge on her, her son taller than she is. That she's amazed is clear in every line of her body. She and Andy don't step nearer or embrace. They just stand talking, and then Dennis sees Christie move to her porch rail, looking down at him bewildered, and he waves at her, a wave that means *I can't explain it.*

Black Dress

Caro calls *"Momentito!"* star-
tled less by the lie than by the Spanish. She arches her back
before sawing the black silk downward, careful to keep her
nails from its tension. Early ninth month: the baby's as definite
a presence as a cat in the lap. Like a cat's, its slow-motion,
kneading exertions only enlarge on a private contentment.
Each gesture, outflung fist or prodding foot, collapses back
into the dreamy fetal tuck. Caro tips her chin up for her
reflection's frank appraisal. Pregnancy panty hose in a particu-

larly dead shade of taupe, belly marbled with veins and budded with her extruded navel, the bones in her ankles indistinct; the doctor lathered his hand and eased her wedding ring from her finger on her last visit, saying, "Women tend to forget this." That visit's sonogram revealed the baby positioned not head down but breech, as cross-legged and adamantly at peace as a little Buddha, its hair candescent grass, its features unfamiliar. Something was wrong with Caro, she was inadequate, she experienced no sharp pang of recognition. The last thing she'd expected was a stranger. Who was that—tilted nose, rosebud pout, comically fat cheek? It dawned on Caro that she'd made one of those private deals that wreaked such havoc with her life. She'd trusted the baby. She would hand her life over to it if in return it would make itself beloved—instantly, completely beloved. *She didn't love it:* a secret she's told no one. (*It:* its sex remained, in the flickering sonogram, secret.) She can stare and stare at her reflection, and not know what she's going to do, and the ultimate disorientation is this: she's supposed to be dressing for a funeral.

So get dressed.

From behind, as she fights the black dress down, comes the creak and hiss of silk stressed too far, and the bind around her belly eases, constriction evaporating miraculously, as at the end of a Braxton Hicks. Her fingertips search the small of her back, though this stance is awkward, her belly jutting hugely. From the kitchen, her husband raises his voice again. "Need me?"

"I'm fine."

"Caro?" His tone says he's looking at his watch.

"Really! Fine!"

Fine. An adrenalized brightening of the senses, careening dismay, her pulse thudding in unusual places, behind her left knee, in the hollow of her throat, even registering in an eyelid as a tic. The exaggerated calm, *First take care of this, then take*

care of that, that would culminate in her suitable appearance at
Katie's funeral eludes her. *Katie's funeral:* the very words seek
to remain an impossibility. *Katie's,* as the possessive for *funeral,*
is alive with thinly vibrating resistance. Katie would hate
having a funeral. Katie's this, Katie's that, "Katie called,"
"Katie forgot her scarf again," and, most usually, at least until
last month's breakup, "Kevin's out with Katie," almost always
absently answered, "Oh, good," guilt briefly releasing its hold
on them, "Good," whether it was Kevin's stepmother or his
father who said it, "Good" because they were grateful, because
Kevin was otherwise so alone, "Good" because whether it was
wise or not they were counting on Katie to relieve Kevin's
depression.

When Caro hazarded, "It's good Kevin has someone," Hart
shot back, "He has me. He has you. It's his mother who
ducked out of his life," yet he knew what Caro meant, he
knew, and, harder for him, he agreed; it was one of those
married exchanges where the original hurtful observation could
have been made by either partner, and the other would have
objected. When they finally met Katie, the question became
I wonder how serious this is, because Katie was serious. Her gaze
met yours with another adult's wry admission of responsibility,
and where did those beautiful manners come from? And who
wouldn't have been persuaded by such composure to think,
Smart, sane, trustworthy?

Her husband calls, "We're waiting," in the brightly conspiratorial tone that signifies, between them, dire emergency.

Hannah should be here. It should be Hannah's job to get
Kevin through this. The five or six times she called, over the
last three days, Hannah seemed to be no comfort to Kevin.
There were long silences, at least on Kevin's side, Caro adroitly
eavesdropping. Hannah should have caught a flight home from
Europe. She repeatedly offered to, and was too easily dissuaded.
Caro will be by far the most marginal person at Katie's funeral,

grief spun out airily thin before reaching her. Describe her—
the dead girl's boyfriend's stepmother—and you see how far
she is from the black vortex of true grief, you see why she feels
nothing, or almost nothing. Sick and dazzled, of course. But
also ill at ease and resentful. All the more reason to appear, if
she has to appear, stricken, silent, courteous, and in black.

Black has failed her, as English sometimes does in emergencies: she couldn't make it do what she wanted. Black would
have helped to counter the ninth-month swagger of her walk.
Caro heaves and wriggles the black dress off. "Rag," she tells
it, "I'll wipe the floor with you." Between her white-knuckled
fists the black rope tenses, knots, resists. She flings it at the
corner.

He calls, "Hey?"

Caro closes her eyes for calm, against dizziness. Let him
get angry. That's not what she fears. She's done enough. She's
done everything he asked, she's been everything he wanted,
and he can't even guess at the extent of her effort. The room
Caro opens her eyes on is, for all its disorder, fraught with
significance. The hairbrush in the rumpled sheets, the bookmark in *Your Baby and Child,* the single high heel stranded
under the chair—none of these are what they appear to be,
random. She brushed her hair while sitting up in bed, half-
asleep but signaling *I'm awake,* because her husband woke, this
day of the funeral, anxious and in need of her. The resolve
behind the bookmark's steady progress through those pages is,
of course, the ambition to be a perfect mother. The high heel
lies where Hart tossed it one night, *the* night, now almost nine
months ago. At first it meant nothing, that high heel lying
where it landed. Ever so slowly it came to mean a great deal.
She's taken pleasure in the decision, repeated countless times
now, to leave that high heel where it is. What Caro loves is
continuity. Continuity is, often, a love rife with absurdities;
it depends, often, on incalculably private shades of significance.
Continuity is the passion of refugees, who seize on it where no

one else, no native, would find it at all. Each night, on the side of the bed near the lamp, she lies waiting. The veining of his forearm, the armpit he isn't aware is graying, the protectively braced balance of his body as he leans across her, spell *safe*. Each night his breathing chest above her, as darkness clicks on, reassures her: *It hasn't happened yet.* She can't say what it is that hasn't happened, or why this phrase should recur, but the night he lies there and asks "Can you get the light?" will count as disaster as surely as if the roof caved in. There are other signs, proofs of betrayal. She'll know them when she sees them. These she fears, so she listens, she observes, she keeps her eyes open, her very clear, dark, undeceived Dominguez eyes—there, in the mirror.

"Is something wrong?"

He can't leave his son. In the days since Katie died, Kevin's scarcely been alone. His father's vigilance has to grate. It's intrusive, demanding, unsubtle, mistrustful.

They must be sitting on either side of the kitchen table, hands folded, shirts and ties facing each other, identically bigknuckled hands, identical lostness, empty coffee cups, spoons resting in saucers. Caro's presence has helped, an innocently third person, a woman, which means, it seems, she knows what to say, and she does know—as when, in a dream, you prove fluent in a language you are naggingly cognizant of never having learned. Still, this was expertise—real or fraudulent, it seemed to be some consolation to Kevin. Caro exacted from Kevin the automaton responses cherished by his father. "I can't." "I'm not hungry." "I don't need anything." "I'm going to bed now, I guess." He wouldn't talk to anyone but her. Inexplicable: she wasn't solicitous with him, not especially. She was conscious of the strangeness of her voice when she asked him if he wanted anything. For some reason, she had his attention. He lifted his eyes, he focused on her. Slowly, but he focused. "No," he said. He said, "Thank you."

Minutes ago, Caro heard the coffee grinder, the single

sound until Hart's voice to break her fascinated comprehension
that the black dress wasn't going to fit. Hart must have stuck
the requisite number of Band-Aids on skinned knees, he must
have stroked Kevin's forehead when he was running a fever,
but from his maladroitness with his son now, you wouldn't
know Hart had ever rocked him calm after a nightmare, and
that Hart should have had even so modest a good idea as coffee
startles Caro. Last night, after Kevin swallowed his Valium at
the kitchen sink, set down his glass, and wandered off to
bed, Hart said, "I think he's basically all right." The only
explanation for this remark is terror. He's terrified for his son.
Terrified people lack judgment, as she well knows.

"Caro?"

From the dresser she takes a glass with what's left of this
morning's milk in it, the hateful obligatory glass a day. Room
temperature, it tastes like sadness. Katie overdosed on her
mother's prescription antidepressants, drugs with names trill-
ingly cheerful—Tofranil, Trilafon, Prozac, Xanax. Katie's
parents recite *We didn't know. We don't know why. We should
have known.*

"Hey?"

Caro nurses her silence. It needs care and feeding, a silence
like that. It exists against the odds, under duress. It's about
to be taken from her.

"Caro?"

Leave me alone, she thinks, and then, meanly, *You have each
other.*

"Sweetie?"

Imagining Katie's funeral, Caro imagines, loomingly and
exclusively, the dead girl's mother, wearing sunglasses, her
lower lip bitten or gnawed, her hands gloved, her manner
drugged, formal, ravaged, remote as an assassin's, all around
her a zone of intolerable reality. It would be dangerous to
disturb that zone by so much as a handshake, a greeting, to
attract from its center a sunglass-blanked gaze, a low, toneless

response or gloved, terrible touch. It would be bad luck. The
baby kicks tentatively, then harder, and Caro's swift sense is
of a soft internal toppling suddenly suspended; again the baby
has stopped before turning head-down. Blunted hope is ex-
hausting. There's nothing mutual about this relationship. The
baby doesn't care enough about its mother to turn one simple
somersault. Caro eases herself to the floor, her back to the wall,
concentrating on shallow breaths that nonetheless bottom out
against her diaphragm. She's starving for a deep breath. Air!
She broods about deep, unimpeded drags like a deprived
smoker fantasizing the next cigarette. *I give and give!* Caro cries
(she doesn't know to whom). *I gave you everything! Now I'm a
naked fat lady!*

"Look at you," her husband says from the doorway.

She leans forward, squatting, trying for balance, belly
swung forward between her stockinged knees, nylon and Lycra
glossy with the strain. The dust under her palms is her own
inattentiveness.

His son waits at the kitchen table in his grim suit, large
hands helplessly embracing an empty coffee cup: Hart instills
his fury at this vision in his voice. "You're not ready."

She says, "I couldn't get my black dress on."

"We had to leave here five minutes ago."

"I'm not going."

When he repeats, "Not going?" his voice is strategically
delicate, entirely alert, though he still hasn't offered a hand.

"I can't come with you. You go, and be on time."

"How long will it take you to get dressed? Let's cut our
losses here. Let's scramble, and we'll make it."

She's shaking her head, looking at the floor: she must look
like a mop of shaking dark hair, from his vantage point. She
says, "I'm not coming at all."

"You're upset. I didn't know. You seemed least—you
seemed fine."

"My dress tore."

He takes it in, the black snarl of the fallen dress and her crouch, and it's then he extends his hand. When she stands, her belly directs its obdurate amplitude at him. She covers the nipples of her breasts shyly, with an arm, fearing they're staring at him.

He says, "Wear another dress."

"There is no other dress."

"What do you mean?"

"That's my only black dress. That *rag*." She understands how long she's been wanting to get rid of the black dress, and she's glad.

"It can't be your only black dress." He starts through her closet, jamming her dresses to one side, then paging back through them in desperation. His suit coat wears the faint luster of strain across the back. He's much taller than she is. In a couple of her dreams he was smaller, so that she could lug him around like a baby. In reality, when he turns, the knot of his tie is at eye level for Caro, an unprecedented knot, neat, businesslike, horrible, choked high under the Adam's apple, so vulnerable in his razor-grazed neck that it excites her pity. His penis does too, sometimes, though she supposes she's not supposed to feel that. When it lies across his thigh after lovemaking, it shrinks in an irregular, wincing fashion that seems entirely sad. In front of his ugly tie, draped across his arm, is the dress she was wearing the night they met.

"No!"

"It's kind of black."

"It's green!" So he has no particular vision of her, high on vodka, catching his eye from across the room? No remembrance, when what he'd called out to her over so many other heads was "You're beautiful"? From a disordered drawer, jutted open from the dresser they share, she takes a bra and struggles to fasten it. Even nine months pregnant, she resists wearing bras. The formality of his tie drives her to this.

"Wear anything, and wear a coat over it. Everyone will be in coats. You don't know, but it's cold."

In coats, huddled around the grave, the spring wind whipping the men's ties, women crossing their arms and holding themselves and then fearing that pose isn't formal enough and letting go, wind catching whatever it can and tugging.

Hart drops the dress that was her, beautiful, the first time he saw her. He seizes the maternity jumper hanging on a bedpost. "Hey! This."

"Just go."

"This dress"—he gives it the light shake he'd like to give her—"will work. I mean, under a coat."

She's backed against the wall, unfinished adobe that grits against her skin like beach sand, bracingly. "It's garish." She's so tired she closes her eyes and yawns.

"Caro, Caro, come on," he says, and closes in on her, his hand sliding behind her, her head not bumping, therefore, but urged backward to rest in that hand even as her face is tilted upward by the other, a fist under her chin, and the weight that seems to melt downward, following her belly's curve, gathering momentum, guided by kicks, is the baby turning over as she's kissed, the circumference of the baby's skull and her pelvis bone grating as they meet, a fit! And sudden lightening, her lungs granted delicious depth, and she has only to wait for the end of this kiss for breath, lovely breath, her life saved, and he asks, taking his mouth away at last, "All right now?" and she gets her breath, and because he's impatient he doesn't wait for her answer but insists, "All right? Can we go?"

"The baby went head-down."

"Good, honey, now come on."

He is so far from the reality of body, of breath, that she can hate him as from a great distance. She wonders what it meant to him, the screaming in the movies they watched, the

distorted faces of the mothers, the fear, and then, what everyone claimed was miraculous, the mucus-streaked scalp bulging
from the warped, impossibly open vagina. Does he think she
isn't going to bleed? If she knew he was going to bleed,
or scream, it would obsess her. He says, "You look better.
Calmer."

"Calmer!"

"Let's get you dressed."

"You're going to have to go without me. See, this has
nothing to do with me."

In the faraway kitchen, the phone rings. It rings twice,
and Hart says, "He's going to answer the fucking telephone,"
and Kevin must have, because it stops ringing. "No, no, no,
no, what fucking luck."

She wants to rest, but she's willing to fight. She doesn't
care what it takes to resist him. She says, "The world didn't
stop because Katie died."

"That means?"

"The phone can ring."

"Caro," he says rapidly, "I don't know why you're who
he's talking to, but you are, you know you are. If you don't
come, it's like saying he shouldn't have trusted you."

She says plainly, "I'm tired."

"I know you're tired."

A tight, compacted popping low in her pelvis distracts
her. Hiccups, maybe brought on by exertion. "The baby has
hiccups," she tells Hart, out of an obscure need to keep him
posted.

"You have to do the right thing." He sighs. "You were so
great until now."

She says, "I didn't mean it. My heart wasn't in it."

He says, "Oh Christ, of course you meant it. It's *this* you
can't mean. Craziness and selfishness you can't mean."

Stubbornly, she shakes her head.

"You're going to have to tell him something. Invent a reason, lie, tell him you're sick, *look* sick. Make him believe you." And he adds "Wear this thing" so angrily that, with abrupt submissiveness, she takes the foolish flowered dress and draws it, in tender yanks and smoothings, down her body, a dress so soft, so utterly accommodating, so evocative of her sisters, having been worn by sister after sister, that Caro sometimes sleeps with it, as she used to sleep in bed with them, the texture of consolation unmistakable. The sister who sent the dress folded a note into it: *Your turn.*

He believes he's got an advantage he should press—also, her resistance still seems unreal to him. "No one will see the dress, Caro. You can wear a coat. We'll all be bundled up."

"I'm not taking the baby to a funeral."

This remark, surely the strangest she's made, rouses him to astonishing tolerance. "All the baby knows is *you*. You're the world to him. The baby's not going to know it's a funeral. You could go to a circus and the baby wouldn't think, *Hey! Clowns! Dancing bears!*"

She closes her eyes, unwilling to hear another word, and then his hand's on her foot. He's urging her to step into her shoes, and she does, opening her eyes. In the mirror, the dress blooms, an exuberant Dominguez dress, the family theory being that the best part of pregnancy is display. She brushes her hair, inconsequentially stalling, and he begins to pick up—Hart, who can wander past fallen underwear and balled-up, dusty socks for months, has taken the high heel from under the chair, and holds it, puzzled.

"Can you please put that back?"

"What?"

"That shoe."

He says "This shoe?" stupidly, and she takes it from him. She tries to replace the shoe in its talismanic spot. She straightens, and toes it farther under the chair, but it's still not right, and she wants to cry. He says, though not roughly, "Come on, O.K.?"

In the kitchen, the darkening downward rush toward the funeral resembles a kind of drunkenness. All of their movements, even hers, seem ill-timed, and when Kevin rises, giving that hunched shrug men give to their jackets to settle them better, he bumps into his father, and his father bumps into her. Everyone says "Sorry" softly. Kevin is wearing his coat, and a muffler. Caro recognizes Katie's black cashmere, often forgotten. Held to the nose, it would still yield up Katie. Caro imagines the kitchen as it will be after they are gone, how it will drift in space, the afternoon lighting the table inch by inch until it lights her cup of tea. The light edging its way across the table, not failing to pick out the grains of sugar in that tiny spill, not neglecting the rim of the spoon, will be the approach of a less terrified sense of reality.

Kevin, unsure why they're not leaving—they should run—takes his cup from the table and places it in the sink, as she's so often asked him and he's never before remembered to do. A shock, china to china, chatters through the dirty dishes heaped there. Caro's mother, in faraway Brooklyn, can hear it. Caro says, "My black dress tore, Kev. I can't go to the funeral. I am so sorry."

He says, "I wondered what was wrong."

She strokes her lurid stomach. "It would be so rude, all these flowers."

"Yeah." This is consent rather than agreement. He's giving her permission to do this awful thing to him, she understands that.

Hart, wearing his winter coat, an ungainly old-mannish gray tweed, slaps at his pockets and concludes, "Kevin, you've got the keys."

The keys hit his father's extended hand, and Kevin gets out of there, letting the wind in, the kitchen door hanging open as it often does, the room flooded with absence. Hart puts his fingers to the bridge of his nose, then digs with his thumbs into the inner corners of his closed eyes with the blanched delicacy of someone wringing at a migraine. When he takes his hand away, his expression is so altered by rue as to be unrecognizable. "I know you're not trying to hurt him."

She says, "How could anyone want to hurt him?"

"Then come to this funeral." He revolves his shoulders restlessly in his overcoat. Her not moving, her simply standing there, is *no,* an amazing *no.*

He crosses their yard in long strides as she studies him from the doorway, wedging the screen door open with her arm, shivering, the forgotten panty hose a sleekly alien texture when she rubs one calf against the other. Surely she looks comical: a Matisse cutout of a person, a big simple outline filled in with flowers, a crude, happily burgeoning shape. The dirty snow in their yard is yielding to grass, and the air smells of thaw. It's broodingly overcast, and windy. She shivers, and just then the neighbors' Lab lopes purposefully across their lawn. Hart dodges, a mistake: the puppy circles, pleased to set this tall, awkward man into a self-protective spin. Hart swings at the dog—enraged, using his fist. The dog snaps. From his raspberry-pink tongue, a little steam wafts; he snaps again. Running, Caro cries out with a vengefulness the dog understands. She attracts his attention, but he's amused. He rolls in the grass from merriment, for defiance, before running home. Hart unclenches his fist and strokes it with his other hand as if it's an animal, a ferret someone handed him, saying, *See if you can calm this down.* His skin seems bright white except where it's patchily flushed, and the wind's rumpled the hair he wanted decorously smooth. They both consider the single muddy paw print on his knee. "He didn't bite me," Hart said.

"When we get to the car, we can work on it with your handkerchief. You have a handkerchief?"

"I have handkerchiefs." When he sees her surprise, he explains. "I thought Kevin might, uh, cry. He hasn't, so far. That we know of."

"I'll walk you."

"You're going to get cold. Go back. I'm fine." He means he can deal with the paw print, but it's her province, clothes and what happens to them; she's not a seamstress's daughter for nothing. She says, "Can I wear your coat?"

Hart likes parking in the woods above the house, near the highway, because this driveway's prone to potholes and is stony enough to be hard on the suspension of his old BMW. She stays out of the mud by walking in the grass, foxtails parting springily and then swatting her knees—last year's weeds, but dense and resilient on this slope. Her hands form fists inside his coat's pockets. Inside the pockets are gloves. These gloves fit *her*. She holds her gloved hands toward her husband. "A student left them behind in class. I'm keeping them to give back."

He falls behind her. He climbs by way of the road rather than its shoulder. He's wagering it's safer that way. She outdistances him because she doesn't mind what happens to her legs or dress or coat. She's surprised to hear him laughing behind her. When she gives him a look over her shoulder, he calls, "You have this Charlie Chaplin walk. What happened?"

"I told you. I can feel the baby's head, kind of, between my legs."

He lags behind. There is Kevin in the car's backseat. When she pulls the front door open, it's not as if she's surprising him, it's as if she's hurting the car—as if it were a single rigid, shining surface she's cracked, like a sheet of ice. She ducks her head into a different, car-scented volume of cold. She remembers how the most ordinary events and gestures, before a funeral, seem unreal, and how hard it is, since this is so, to judge what is happening. She remembers her mother sitting bolt upright beside her, taking Caro's hand and drawing it toward herself, beginning to prise, with her thumbnail, at a scab on the back of Caro's hand, picking at it and then, fascinated and unaware, resting her fingertip in the blood welling up, Caro unwilling to withdraw her hand and wake her mother but ashamed that she was bleeding at her father's funeral, that there was blood, that her mother could look and see *blood*. She feared her father was embarrassed. Caro was five: she trusted her father to be elsewhere than in that wooden box, and to be aware of what was happening at his funeral.

Caro yearns, absurdly longs, to tell Kevin this story. He would understand. How often, with what painful patience, she's explained herself to his father, and to Kevin when she had to, but she hasn't yet managed to tell them the necessary things—how recklessly she's left them all unsaid, and how hugely sad they make her now. Because she is finally sad, she climbs into the car. Hart closes the door behind her, and gets in behind the wheel. Wet leaves, with a sparse, blown randomness, cling to the windshield. The light through the glass is as mobile as if they're underwater, shifty, cool light with brighter spots, sliding radiance. Hart says, to take the curse off, "Now the damn car won't start," but it starts, idling in a ragged, percolating purr. He is talking to the car when he says, "I knew you'd come through for me."

She says, "I'm really cold."

At Kevin's touch, she jumps. Katie's muffler spills softly over her shoulder, and she catches cashmere, and winds it around her throat, knowing Kevin will take that for thanks. The car rolls sluggishly into the tight curve where the drive feeds into the two-lane highway, and as they nose out from the woods, Hart says, "We're fine."

With some effort she latches her seat belt. "How are we fine?"

"We'll get there in time. We won't be the last to the

funeral." He sets his watch fast to deceive himself. She used to love them, the tricks with which he mitigated his own carelessness. She loved them as long as she didn't believe he was a truly careless person. Now, however she loves him, she has to recognize: he can be careless in big and little things, he can listen to her and not hear her, he can forget what she looked like the first night he saw her. He says, "Kevin? Who was on the phone?"

"Nobody."

"Nobody?"

"You know, you say hello, the other person says nothing."

"Oh," his father says softly.

"I said *hello, hello, hello, hello, hello, hello*. I couldn't stop saying *hello*. I said it maybe fifty times."

"Kevin." His father doesn't want extravagance, not even now.

"A dozen."

"It doesn't mean anything, Kev."

Kevin says, not wanting to hurt his father but telling him the truth, "Saying *hello, hello, hello,* to no answer. See, there is someone there, whether they talk to you or not. So they know you were desperate to talk to them. I think they should know that."

His father says, "So whoever they were, they know that."

They're quiet, all three, until Kevin says, "You're not supposed to believe she's dead, but I believe it. You don't have to think I'm crazy or confused."

This is the changed world, winding highway, canyon wall, chiseled rimrock and precariously balanced black volcanic boulders, then the grays, alternately brilliant and dull, of low, blowing clouds, the kind that might rain in an hour, or not at all. When Hart says, "Want the heater?," Caro says, "No," realizing then that she should still be cold. For now it's so sweet, being warm, that she buttons her coat as far as it will go over her belly, thinking that this is how people dress after natural disasters, fires and earthquakes, in odds and ends, rummaging through relief boxes, stunned to find themselves whole, not caring that everything comes from strangers. She's warm, though nothing she's wearing belongs to her at all. Or else it belongs to her entirely, warming her completely in the interval between the giving and the giving back.

Ciudad Juárez

The Subaru's air-conditioning purrs arduously, pitted against the one-hundred-and-one-degree radiance of Texas, turning the dust on its dash to platinum lint and burning twin suns into the big black lenses hiding Tom's wife's eyes. Tatters of orange peel, a Styrofoam cup whose crescent indentations are the repeated nickings of Tom's wife's thumbnail, a foxed map folded to the Rio Grande, a tiny quartz arrowhead—bird point—from the desert beyond the last rest stop: the litter, cumulatively somehow depressing, of five hours' conversationless travel. Her silence isn't aimed at him, Tom knows. They're not a couple to nurse mutual incomprehension in silence; they're more likely to expect too much of each other, and so, after a little oblique study, he decided to leave Nina alone.

Ten miles back, she'd caught his wrist and slanted it toward herself to read his watch, and then, he'd thought, she would say something; she'd say, "It's two o'clock," or "It's getting late," in the faintly marveling tone she reserves for that observation, but she'd said nothing after all. In essence, despite touching him, she had not felt compelled to acknowledge his existence. She'd simply taken possession of his wrist. For years they had done such things back and forth without their meaning anything. She had straightened his tie, or he had brushed strands of hair from the corner of her smile. He can remember using a fingertip to rub lipstick from one of her front teeth, the left, which minutely, endearingly, overlaps the other, his favorite imperfection in her body. Just now her clasp was too light to alter the peacefulness with which his hand lay on the wheel. Her touch was utterly familiar, light, practical, dismissive, quick. It made him nervous. Yet they can't make each other nervous; it's a possibility that vanished from their marriage long ago. They're so deeply unselfconscious with each other, in fact, that it's not even clear that she "borrowed" his wrist, or "took temporary possession" of it. It's as if she read her own watch, really, moving her own arm slightly to do so, thinking nothing of it. Her touch couldn't have been more neutral, so why did he experience it as so suddenly, exquisitely sexual? If a stranger, someone he'd never seen before, touched him unexpectedly, wanting only to learn the time, he would feel this intruded on, this moved. How can Nina's touch be as disturbing as a stranger's?

A generous interpretation: sex, sensing a vacuum, nimbly presents itself as a way of making contact.

Here, on the map, the Rio Grande's blue hairline intersects the black dashes of the Mexican border, but if the river's down there, it's lost in the glare of sunstruck sand. The American traffic slows for the bridge. On its far side the sentry boxes that should house Mexican Customs are boarded shut, spray-painted in slashes and scrawls naming couples and sexual acts. Nina asks, "Nobody stops us?"

"Hey, they want us," Tom says, relieved. Garbo talks. She goes further, twisting in her seat belt to report, of the baby behind them in his car seat, "Still out. Thumb in his mouth."

"Is he getting enough air-conditioning?"

She leans over the seat back to not-quite-touch the baby's forehead. "I think so."

The books say parents should spend time alone with each twin, but this is almost the first occasion Wills and Griffin have been separated. Griffin has been left in Santa Fe with the boys' sitter, Carmelita Diáz, who was hardly in the door before she cocked a confident hip for Griffin to straddle and told Nina to leave now, please, before the *hijito* knew what was happening. If Nina had only trusted her with Wills, too, this weekend would surely be easier.

⌈Juárez is, first, a small park of dead grass edged with dying palms and an asphalt spur where drivers lean against their cabs, surveying the crush of tourist traffic⌋ Tom could park the Subaru, safe in its shiny, uninsured Americanness, and bargain for a cab. Too late. Traffic carries him past the turnoff. His sunglasses are so clouded with baby fingerprints that he hands them to Nina to burnish on her skirt, hoping that her gesture will clear his mind as well.

What he wants wiped away is a scene: himself, growling like an airplane, aiming a spoon at Griffin's mouth, while in his high chair Wills yelled, "Da! Da-da!" Nina came up behind, putting an arm around Tom's neck, weighing against him until he knew from the tightening helplessness of her hold

that something was wrong and asked, "O.K., what?" She said,
"I am," and he had to look from the brilliant blue slip of
litmus paper into her eyes, also brilliant, reading there that
until he too saw this proof, she had not believed it. "Oh,
Nina, no," he said. "It can't be right."

"It is right. I knew anyway. I feel like before."

Griffin threw his bowl to the floor, and oatmeal splattered
Nina's bare feet. She bent to wipe them clean with the sleeve
of her sweatshirt, and he couldn't see her face for the fall of
her hair when she said, "I can't have another baby."

"I know."

He was agreeing, but she went on as if he hadn't, her voice
as furious as when they quarreled. "These two take everything.
I'd be gone. I'd disappear. My life would be gone."

He turns his head briefly for Nina to slide his glasses back
on. Her touch smarts on his nose, burned from the few desert
minutes in which, walking away from the rest stop into an
arroyo whose air had the sick shimmer of gasoline-tainted heat,
past the inevitable charred tires and shattered glass, he'd found
the quartz point. It had a fresh whiteness like salt's, and was
weightless as a contact lens, ancient, intact, still pristinely
sharp. He'd wished he could walk farther—an archaeologist's
constant impulse—but Nina was waiting, and he hadn't worn
his baseball cap. Usually he's pretty self-protective. The sun
at his dig in Chaco Canyon has an X-ray intensity. He's in the
sun a lot. Gone a lot. Nina's needed him, and he just hasn't
been home. The sleepless intensity of the twins' first ten
months fell almost entirely on her. This time there's anguish
in the commonplace recognition that he could have been more
careful.

"This traffic," Nina says vaguely.

"Want to stop?"

"Where? And it would wake Wills."

"How's he doing?"

Absurd to ask for the second time in five minutes, but again Nina reassures him, "He's really out. He's fine," the tenderness in her tone referring backward, as she assumes his anxiety does, to ten months ago, to a relief so pure that time has scarcely diluted it. His brother was fine, but Wills, too small, spent his first week in neonatal care, heels periodically pricked for blood, fists small as violin scrolls, chapped skin distressingly red against sterile cotton; even his mewing sounded raw, fetal, exposed. Nina would not touch him. The nurses said this was not an uncommon response. It wasn't unusual, even, that Nina didn't want to name him. Attachment, at this point, seemed too dangerous, but a touch or a name would be good signs. Under the heat lamp's mild aura the newborn waited, silver disks taped to his chest, wires flexing minutely with his breathing, illumined dials presiding, until one night Nina, stepping cautiously across the trailing wires, stroked his cheek. His head jerked, his eyes opened to her gaze. In a corner, there was a rocking chair. The nurses whispered back and forth. Wills gained two ounces—three— to weigh four and a half pounds. Rocking, Nina looked up at Tom as if she didn't remember him. The baby that might not make it was always crying, Nina's head bent until her lips grazed his hair, repeating the name she'd given him: Will, to add, with each repetition, a feather's weight to the side opposite death. Tom was stunned, when once a vial of the baby's blood was carried past him, by the wish to cry out.

Ten days, then two weeks. Their neighbor Carmelita Díaz had moved into their house, taking over Griffin. Though he needed a way to pass the time, there were only so many phone calls Tom could stand to make, so many quarters he could stand to send *chinging* into the pay phone in the corridor. Once as he waited there, about to dial his home number again, a nightgowned girl in labor approached, wheeling her IV stand, stopping to brace herself against a wall when a contraction hit.

Tom found himself wanting to ask, as her breathing eased, if he could do something, get her something, but his T-shirt was sweated through under the arms; he probably smelled of his own sick tension. He hung up the phone. He went to the window: outside was a July evening, birds skimming past, cumulonimbus clouds boiling up over the Sangre de Cristos. Tom leaned his forehead and forearm against glass alive with the permanent, mute, scarcely perceptible tremor of air-conditioning, while the girl, with small moans, rode out another contraction.

In the end, they were lucky: Wills weighing five pounds, they went home, but the emotional constellation formed in neonatal care subversively persists. It's Wills whose hold on his parents is the more potent and infatuated, Griffin who chose to wean himself abruptly, biting Nina whenever she unbuttoned for him. Letting himself in one evening, wondering at the silence, Tom padded in stocking feet through the house to find Nina asleep in a pile of dirty laundry, the naked twins crawling around her. As Tom caught Wills, Griffin peed, crowing, on Tom's favorite shirt. It was an hour before Tom got both boys bathed and in bed, and still Nina lay dreaming in a welter of sheets and shirts and small overalls.

"Did we lose a dirty diaper in here?" Tom asks. "No," Nina says shortly. A lick of red hair, loosed from her chignon, clings to Nina's nape, and her freckles are out in force. [Six lanes of idling American cars are the Avenida de la Revolución. Neon ice in cones: their vendor, a pretty girl ducking to Tom's window, smiles brightly to show missing front teeth.] Nina shakes her head, and the girl is gone. Glacierlike, the glittering cars grind forward in concerted, decisive inches. Nina bites her thumbnail in rapid, critical clicks. What her ob-gyn in Santa Fe gently told Nina was that abortions are not considered safe before six weeks. She was—the sonogram proved—only four weeks along. The wait is now almost behind them. The abortion is scheduled for Monday, the day after tomorrow, in Santa Fe, but they couldn't have stood waiting at home.

When a street opens to their right, Tom tries it. "How hot do you think it is?" Nina says. "Do you know where we're going?"

"*Is* there a dirty diaper lost in here?" Tom demands, with such miserable rudeness that she scrabbles underfoot even as he chooses street after street for their increasing emptiness, and the buildings on either side grow smaller, meeker, older, and more foreign, their plaster no longer pink or turquoise but dusty ocher, no neon advertising *cerveza,* no iron flourishes. When Nina sits up, having found nothing, the world is poor and shut against them.

"I hate this," she says.

"Well, we're lost." Desperately, he's trying to reconstruct the turns he made, each on the spur of the moment, no logic linking them, when Nina says, "Look," and a bicycle whisks alongside agilely as a trotting dog. The bicycle's crouching child, a wing of black hair falling just shy of his eyes, asks Tom, "Where to?" This phrase exhausts the boy's English and he can only, pitched forward optimistically over the handlebars, wait on Tom's answer; he does this by gracefully, agreeably coasting, adding not a pedal's stroke of pressure to his sweet selling job.

Nina leans across Tom, her hand on his leg, and asks in Spanish to be led to the big shopping *mercado, por favor.* The bicycle flicks away, down an even narrower street, and Tom asks, "Did we have a deal?"

"He's showing off," Nina says, "but yes."

"What are you getting us into?" Tom wrenches the Subaru into the turn, but it's tight, and he's glancing back to check the fender when Nina cries "No!" in time for Tom to brake, the Subaru jolting to a stop, the boy inches before them, holding up his arms to show no harm was done. Nina calls, *"¡Oye, chico, demasiado cerca!"*

"Can you get him back? I'm going to get out and scream at him. That was fucking dangerous."

"In what language?"

"He'd get it."

"He thought he'd lost his rich customers," Nina says, "plus he's a little macho."

"Now where are we?" Tom asks, because this street is wider, opening into another, where spandex-legged girls balance on high heels and iron arabesques guard shop windows. Here it is again, the blazing Avenida, traffic locked tight, and Tom hammers the wheel with a fist.

"It's O.K., it's O.K.," Nina says.

"How is this O.K.?"

"So he made a mistake. He can't be more than ten."

"I should never have followed him," Tom says, and then, "Did you notice his hand?"

"His hand?"

"He's got it bandaged in something filthy."

"All I saw was his face. His face is beautiful."

"I haven't given him a dime," Tom says, "and he's sitting out there for us in that sun."

Tremors of movement run toward them through the traffic. The boy waits for an opening to the right, taking it so fast that Tom pops his turn signal and begs over his shoulder for a way in. Granted, by an Isuzu pickup; Nina waves thanks, and the boy shoots away again, another lane over, behind a refrigerator truck.

"I'm going to lose him again if he's not careful."

"Pay attention."

"This is his fault," Tom insists, because it's infuriating, the adroit bicycle, the blocked traffic unpredictably spurting ahead, the glare he's squinting into when Nina cries out. Something thumps into them and spills with a raggedly rolling momentum across the hood and down. He has automatically slowed and stopped, he has even assured himself from the rearview that he won't get hit from behind, because while his fear is great, it has endowed Tom with the lucidity of adrenaline, plowing him through a single vast thought at a time as everything around him shudders, slows, and stalls, and the beautiful life he has lived until this moment breaks off and floats away.

Nina pleads, "Don't go," in a tone so passionate and clear that he listens to her; he stops, thinking she knows something he's missed, but of course she doesn't, and though he hates leaving her now he answers in a voice as clear as her own, "I killed him," and climbs from the car to crouch at what should be the body of the boy and is, instead, *instead,* a khaki duffel from which, by lifting and violently shaking, he spills five pairs of boots, their leather superheatedly slick in the sun, unreal, real. From nearby cars, he is called a whore's son, an idiot, a *chingal,* but he feels an exquisite high, setting each miraculous boot onto its sharp-toed shadow. Nina is squatting, asking, "Are you all right?"

"I'm wonderful."

"Please don't lose it. Not now."

They stand up together. He takes her sunglasses off for the first time that day to tell her eyes "I love you."

"I know."

"How are you? Are you O.K.?"

"I'm fine," she says, but the bearded guy who's climbing out of the Mercedes in front of them, having heard Tom's question, feels obscurely bound to repeat it, and when Nina doesn't answer, he tries Tom. "How are you? How is she?" He's wearing a Dodgers cap, and mirror shades; little of his expression shows. "I'm a doctor," he adds.

"What's with the boots?" Tom asks, over the symphony of horns and insults.

"I bring my boots down here to get them reheeled. A Mexican guy does it for me. Hospital floors wear them right down. We're having one hell of a fight, and she says she can't stand it, and chucks these boots out the window before I can stop her. Throws the back door right open. She's always throwing things of mine away. Sometimes I come home after a long day to find two dozen shirts on the lawn, flung all over, getting rained on by the sprinklers. Next time we come down to Juárez it's for a divorce." He shakes his head heavily. "My insurance is taking care of this." He flicks through a satiny black wallet for a card.

"Good," Tom says.

Nina says, "We're leaving. I'm driving," hooking her sunglasses; Tom had forgotten he had them. She tells the bearded doctor, "We never want to hear from you. Never, got it?"

The guy appeals to Tom—"You should take this"—but Nina drops the card into the street. Nina drives, and either Juárez does not confuse her or the accident has, oddly, cleared her mind. A small street with one pretty restaurant in its middle appears for her. They park under palms. Inside, the restaurant is wonderfully cold and dark. Nina deciphers the handwritten menu while Wills peels cellophane from a saltine. The waitress stops to admire Wills's corn-silk blondness before liberating him from his high chair and waltzing him away.

"I should trust this, but I don't," Nina says, and follows. From the kitchen comes high, ecstatic Spanish—a baby party. The fuss is even worse when both twins are together. Tom agrees with himself that he's light-headed and should eat. The waitress reappears, alone but bearing huge plates. Tom tarts up his Tecate with salt and lime. In the poster above him, the bull's head is lowered, the cape soars out, and the matador's golden backside is beautiful as a girl's.

"It's nice you didn't go crazy back there with that guy,"
Nina says, returning to buckle Wills into his chair.

"I was so scared it was that kid I hit."

"You told me, 'I killed him.' "

"I remember "

" 'I killed him.' "

"Well, didn't you think that?"

"I didn't think it was him you hit, no. You weren't being
rational."

"So I'm the one who panics," he marvels, meaning he very
slightly doubts her word. He doubts he went through those
frantic emotions alone.

"Do you know that story Paula tells?" Paula is a friend of
theirs, an anthropologist working in Cuzco; he nods, and she
goes on. "The earthquake wakes her in the middle of the night,
and she grabs her husband, and they're flat in the bed with
fear, and it's this long, long time for them before they think
of the baby in his crib across the room."

"And?"

"Don't be like that. Don't expect me to be like that."

"I still don't understand."

"I mean"—she sets her fork down—"Paula fears for herself. That's natural. You feared for that boy. That's natural.
All I think of is Wills right behind us in his car seat, strapped
in, safe, quiet, O.K., and my fear stops right there, and that's
natural. I'm not going to judge the way any of us responds to
things. In what people feel, they're alone."

"But that's so lonely," Tom says. "I couldn't stand to
believe that."

"You want to know the first time I even remembered that
boy? When we got back into the car and traffic had carried
him away, I thought, 'He's not going to get paid.' Then I felt
sorry for him."

Tom says, "His instinct would be not to hang around
trouble. The cops could come."

Wills oils a piece of avocado with saliva and skates it around his tray. Nina says, "Eat it, Wills. Eat it. Eat it." Wills says, "Da fix," and sweeps it to the floor. He trades stares with his mother, angelic sweetness on his side, maternal inscrutability on hers. Nina says, "I want to go home *now.*"

Under a half-moon, the border has backed up into a vast plain of taillights in which the only moving things are beggars. Tom hangs his hand out the window, but when a crippled girl lifts twenty dollars from his fingers and seesaws away on her crutches, he feels nothing, no more than if the wind had blown it away. U.S. Customs is the distant waist of the hourglass, letting a red grit of taillights tick through. In the seat behind him, Nina nurses Wills, being discreet because now and then a beggar leans right into the window, having observed that the driver is vulnerable, is guilty, will give. Though Tom empties his wallet, Nina says nothing. She doesn't say, "Save at least something." Nursing, Wills fools around, cooing to the breast. "I wish I was you," Tom tells Nina.

"Why?"

"Because all you do is sit there, and he gets what he needs."

Tom keeps the Subaru nuzzled up against the rear of an old Ford pickup. Four men are sleeping there, dirty straw hats slanted down. When the truck reaches Customs, the inspector lowers his clipboard and lets his flashlight wake the men. He orders them out. They clamber down, standing ashamed in the concentrated light of waiting cars.

"These guys could take forever," Tom tells Nina. "They're Mexican, crossing on a big night. I'd be suspicious."

"Of what?"

"Don't you worry that Carmelita's husband comes and goes this way?"

Carmelita's husband periodically disappears back to his

Oaxacan hometown. "Sure," Nina says. "But he's paid somebody here. He knows how to get away with it. I'm not even
sure she'd mind if he went to jail."

"The last time he was home, I could hear them making
love," Tom says

"What do you mean, you could hear them?"

She's not going to like this part. "It was when you had the
flu and she stayed over. They were on the floor of the babies'
room."

"My God," Nina says. "She's fired."

"They weren't loud. It was just their voices, talking."

"Were they happy?"

He thinks. "Yes, they were happy. I think so." He waits
a moment. "Nina, we'll be happy again. We'll be fine."

"You don't wish you were me," she says.

She's still behind him, so he can't see her. "Why don't I?"

"You couldn't stand to feel what I'm feeling."

The four men swing themselves in, the pickup rolls forward, and Nina and Tom are asked what country they're citi-
zens of. The flashlight splashes the backseat bright as daylight
and starts Wills crying, and he cries as they're waved through,
he cries all the way through an El Paso abandoned for Saturday
night, he cries at the desk under the disapproving gaze of the
clerk and up the elevator of the hotel, the first hotel Tom
noticed, Nina holding Wills and humming against his head.
Somebody, some drunk, has punched all the buttons, and
Wills cries in gusting wails until finally, as the elevator doors
break apart on a last genteelly lit and carpeted corridor, he
quiets.

Tom lugs bags around and settles them in while Nina
bathes Wills. When Tom looks in on them, the mother leaning
into the tub, the baby standing up sucking a washcloth, Nina
yawns. "I can't stay awake," she says. "Please stay awake," he
says, "we have to talk," but once she's put Wills down, singing

him through his resistance to yet another strange place, she drags her T-shirt off, her shoulder blades set tight with fatigue, her bare back brilliant in the moment before the bathroom door closes. Fresh water is run into the baby's leftover bath, a hairbrush clicks down against the sink, and then Tom hears her gratefulness as she enters the water, the skid of her bottom against porcelain, her chin tilted up, he imagines, so that her head can rest against the rim. While still distantly conscious of needing to stay awake, he's asleep. He's almost asleep. Wills whimpers and is shushed. Nina's in bed, then, and to his surprise she wants to make love. When they're done, she's still lying across him, breathing past his ear into the pillow; she says, "Sadness. Just such sadness"—answer to a question he can't remember asking. She kisses him before he can say "What?" His tongue finds the imprecision in her front teeth, that minute edge of overlap, and maybe because he's so tired he thinks something strange: if they were buried just like this, then someone unearthing Nina's skull could see that same flaw a hundred, a thousand, years from now, could even touch it, could be that far from now and not know what to feel.

Earth to Molly

A woman was reading, and a man was watching her read, on a train to Wales when the pages of her book turned soft gray and disappeared, the gray brief-lived and the dark after that very dark, though not complete—not *night,* but deep enough that when she glanced up, all the small points of orientation she had unconsciously collected over the last several hours had vanished. *Not there, not there, not there*—the elderly man's hat, the child's handprint floating on a window, the becalmed perspective of receding seat backs, gone. Molly was lost. She was to imagine, later, the expression on her face, inasmuch as it could be perceived in the dark. Very likely he could see better than she could see, in the dark.

He leaned forward to touch her knee, and remained leaning forward as they slid through the series of resonant echoes, Molly explaining to herself, *Train. Tunnel. Nothing's wrong.* If he'd touched her hand instead of her knee, the gesture would have been reassuring in the way he meant, or mostly meant; nothing would have changed between them. She wouldn't have found herself holding her book to her chest so that she could lean toward him. His lank black forelock fell to the outer corner of an eyebrow, and because his short beard grew close around his mouth, his mouth seemed to deserve attention— as if it were just luck you'd seen it, that mouth. She understood she'd been aware of his mouth all along. He existed interest- ingly—partially; in glints, in guessed-at contours—in the dark. *Train.* She'd forgotten she was on a train. They kissed, balancing, having to balance, making minute concessions to this distraction, to their almost awkwardness. She absorbed this reality: their teeth, their tongues, the frankly sour grown- male taste, his breathing, the surprising fingertips with which he steadied her chin as faint concussions or tremors ran upward through them, running through them in sync, no lapse, no gap, an identical, subtly sexual jarring, not *them,* not their doing, something that was happening to them, neither of them responsible, in the dark.

Light was sliding back into place down the length of the carriage as they leaned back into their opposite seats. Echoes died behind them not all at once but raggedly, as an orchestra finishes tuning. Drifted leaves made a tortoiseshell ground against which the bare trees flashed sharp-twigged and cold. The speed of the train disturbed nothing, not a leaf out there. The woods didn't look very *well.* They were cold English

woods—or was this Wales? She could ask, but he'd switched
his attention from her to the window. He was that graceful.
She didn't like herself for the voluptuousness of her relief, a
big velvet emotion she could wrap up in, and didn't like him
because he could so easily leave her alone, because he wasn't
immediately intent on the kiss's meaning something. He
wasn't intent on her at all but was gazing out the window with
a sadness so stark and unqualified that it was, even in an
unknown and therefore relatively unreadable face, plainly
sadness.

Here it was, the hurt like that when either of her parents,
distracted from her, grew suddenly sad. For reasons she
couldn't fathom, such sadness excluded her. However inadvertently, sadness, or even occasionally a mood as minor as
disappointment, as supposedly fleeting as that, had caused
her parents to seem elusive. This sadness proved to her what
she was always forgetting in their presence, that she neither
understood nor knew them completely. An intolerable aspect of childhood was that your parents could so swiftly and
irresponsibly provoke in you a feeling of the most intense
isolation.

She didn't want to contemplate fear of abandonment in
regard to someone she didn't know, but she hated it that he
was leaving her alone. Molly ridiculed herself indulgently,
using Joe's kid's slang, *Earth to Molly,* and began to feel better.
Where there had been woods there were now houses, strict,
small, brick, abrupt, their late-fall gardens walled in brick.
His face stood out with a powerful distinctness in the last of
the sun through the window. He let a long arm lie along the
back of his seat. She imagined, in the slightly self-conscious
line of that arm, the press of her own shape, and wondered if
she were wrong.

What she hated about starting something was how often
you had to wonder if you were wrong. You had to know

someone incalculably well before you were sure—wrong, right, *I know where I am with you.*

That wasn't all she hated about starting something. She didn't, in the first place, *want* something. Possibly she was wrong in the most sweeping sense, wrong to have come to England, though: he could live without her ten days, Joe said. They'd been sleeping together with a licentiousness that felt charmed, trying to conceive a child. In Albuquerque International, in the ladies', she found she'd gotten her period. Molly had been enough of a doubter to pack Kotex. They'd been trying for five—now six—months. The interesting thing was that Joe was outside, waiting to ride up the escalator with her to her gate, and she hadn't told him.

In England, nothing was very clear to her except that she wasn't really willing to read from her book again. She was going to have to, of course—this was a book tour, intricately worked out. She dreamed of losing the book, dreamed the usual dream of nakedness before an audience, but this was worse, and new, this resistance to being herself—the Molly of her poems; they were that kind of poems—in front of another auditorium of peaked British faces set at strict interest. The alternately shrewish and winsome malice manifested in their book-reviewing, she was sure it was there as they listened. Audacity here worked on a much smaller scale, in increments of irony, refinements of accent. Who was she, maladroit, presumptuous, confessional, to read them such poems? When the director of the hall—was it called a union? An arts center?— where she was supposed to read in Wales met her at dinner last night in London, and told her they were to be on the same train tomorrow, she'd been relieved to find herself taken under someone's wing. In a sense, she handed over the burden of Molly—her awkwardness, her neurotic tallying of her mis-

takes, the light (becoming manic) of insomnia in her eyes. He
did fine. He fed her, got her things onto the train, and instructed her not to mind him but to read if she liked. To *read,*
in front of somebody else? He was sure she must be tired with
meeting people, making conversation, and being constantly
flattered. His name was David, and when Molly told him he
was being wonderful to her, he laughed and said he was wonderful to everyone. Are you? Why are you? He said it was
his job.

"Poets," he'd said; he'd grinned—"like a lot of flattery."
"Do I?"
"You're far too intelligent for that."

Inside her bag were copies of her book, a self-protectively
sexy dress to wear to the lectern, silver earrings that were a
good-luck gift from Joe. Also in the overhead rack, rattling
along, lay the cheap folding umbrella bought at the last minute
before boarding the train from an Indian in a tatty black jacket.
Over his upper lip, defining it, the Indian wore a feminine
eyebrow of lustrous black hair. To persuade Molly, he'd sent
umbrellas flaring open one after the other with the *whomp
whomp whomp* of beaten rugs until zoomed-open umbrellas
lolled and rocked by their feet and passersby had to navigate
around them. She chose, and when she gave the vendor the
wrong sum he cried out, delighted with her for having erred
in one of the thousand rapid-fire exchanges he made his living
by. He belonged here, she did not. Her error had dug his
immigrant's finger- and toeholds a little deeper. David was
amused, though not in any protective or possessive way—
keeping his distance, but amused by her.

"Our stop." He was collecting their bags. Climbing out
into the rain, Molly opened her umbrella, dodging sooty litter
blown along the platform. She tried to angle the umbrella to
shelter them both, but before long, David's hair was dripping.
The row of wet pillars they walked alongside had been graffitied

in driven scrawls less spangled and artful than she was used
to. David stopped. "I want that bird," he said, of a rusty rag
somehow flung across the rain-glittering front of the engine.
David waved to the engine's lofty window. He was going to
jump. An arm waved from the cab: *Go.* Maybe it was *Go.*
Nobody's head stuck out to confirm this. He would have to
be fast. He jumped neatly. He was deep in the alley the tracks
ran down, trapped between high, soot-blackened cement walls.
He should not have trusted the wave of an arm with his life.
In the wind, Molly's umbrella kept wanting to block her view
of him, so she collapsed it and let it flap to the pavement and
was at once as wet as David, drenched, sick with crazy tenderness toward his body, for the particular cowlicky wetness of
his sleek dark hair. Molly was a stranger witnessing a child
running out in front of a car—immediate frantic *I'll do anything*
love. He was looking at her from that black depth. He needed
her to take the bird so that he could hike himself back onto
the platform. It had taken—what?—thirty seconds? She bent,
her hair raining in his face, so that David laughed, handing
up a light, uninhabited bundle. She folded its wings shut.
They folded inward with a starchy, slightly mechanical resistance, unexpected. The long, black-striped fawn-and-copper
tail, whatever the bird had gone through, was unbroken. She
touched the breast—baby hair—as, using both hands, he
swung himself up, said "Thanks," and took the bird from her.
"You're not going to eat that." "Why not? It's only had its
neck broken. It's been quite cold. Not dead long, either." He
carried it through needling rain Molly slitted her eyes against,
realizing, when she was an awkward distance away, that she'd
forgotten her umbrella. In the deserted parking lot, his was a
small car stranded in harsh light. Though both of them were
soaking, he dried the pheasant with an old sweater before
bundling it in newspaper and tucking it in against their bags,
lodged tightly together in the trunk.

Now here was a bad moment, Molly folding herself into the MG on the left, the wrong, side of him, attracted to him; his car was so disheveled and cozy, so rapidly making itself warm, that it was as if he'd turned a key and let her into his house. Manuscripts, soiled clothes, pamphlets, and old mail had slid together in haphazard heaps. There were even pebbles, as from a beach, so dull you wonder why they mattered. No woman's things. Molly was careful—not a glove, not a feminine slant to the handwriting on any of the letters. His dark-lashed eye was socketed in shadow, his cheekbone had a fine grain like an eggshell's, in contrast to the imposing orderly sleekness of his beard. Rain glittered in the headlights. He read Cymric to her from street signs and shop windows, plying Molly—she thought—with a sense that all this strangeness could please and amuse, that she must not sit there with her arms around herself feeling tired and misplaced.

When she understood he was hunting through the dark streets of his city for someplace to eat, she asked, "Is it all right if we—if you take me to the hotel?"

"To your hotel? You're not ravenous, then?"

"Nervousness. I can't eat before readings. I never can." This last, though it was a lie, was to make it clear that nervousness wasn't caused by him.

"You must eat" was all he said. He'd tilted her chin while they kissed, too, to suit himself: she didn't protest.

The place he took her to was Indian and garish, and settled across the wood-grain Formica table from each other they were a couple. He dried his beard with his sleeve, grinning at her like a fox from a hole as he did so. He could have been her lover. His conviction that she was interested in his least gesture (as she was) said so, pleasantly. Even as Molly tried to shake off her awareness of how they appeared, it was confirmed in the once-over of their waitress, a fifteen-year-old whose hair had been cramped back from her temples by plastic butterflies.

The sturdy way she set her legs apart, in her short skirt, was flirtation, but it seemed ingeniously to include Molly as well as David. The waitress knew who David was, and liked his coming in from the rain with someone, dripping wet. She told Molly in detail what each dish was and how hot it would be, simply to spend time leaning over Molly's shoulder toward the menu.

"Quite a performance," Molly said when the girl was gone. *Better than me,* she thought. *Surer of herself.* Molly was jealous.

"Sheila," he said, naming the girl. He kept tapping his spoon against his lower lip, ready to laugh. "Nothing much in Sheila's future, I'm afraid."

"You don't know," Molly said, thinking of the girl's energy.

"I know," he said, thinking what she was pitted against.

They'd silenced each other with this disagreement.

"Tell me about your poems. What comes first."

"First?"

"Image? Emotion?" The spoon ticked iambs against Formica. "A train you catch?"

"Landscape."

He laughed. "Not an answer I've had before."

"New Mexico." She hurried; she wanted no lapse in his love of what she was saying; she wanted to be good. "We have a house set over an arroyo, and on the arroyo's other side are hills, and, after that, mesas." She sculpted the house—two-storied, tin-roofed—in miniature, aware suddenly how dear it was to her: a sharp emotion, and oddly timed. Joe lived in that tiny house of air. Guilt. "Tell me why you're here. In Wales."

"I saw Wales when I was a child. I knew then: I was coming back. I can't leave now. I've even tried, once or twice."

Food came. Molly devoured fragrant curried chicken, fawn sauce ladled over white rice, baby-food in texture but spiked

with heat. "You never eat before a reading?" he teased. "Do
you never drink before a reading either?"

"I can't."

Tympani, a drizzling beat, and an eerie disembodied
wailing: Sheila reappeared, dimpling, for their approval. She'd
put romantic music on. As if they were her parents, she wanted
them to love each other. David's knee rested against Molly's.
He ordered a bottle of wine. David listened to the music.
"Somebody's getting their throat cut for love," David said.

At the hotel, really a shabby bed-and-breakfast, the landlady,
pinching her upper lip in displeasure at having to hoist herself
from her chair, let Molly into her room and left her with the
key. The landlady was a long time retreating down the hall.
The dolor of her tread, with its brooding pauses, was not
eavesdropping but arthritis. Molly was sorry for having needed
her to climb the stairs, but of course the old woman complained
her stiff-legged way up them all the time, showing lodgers to
their rooms. Why, oh why, would anyone spend the night
here? A prickly gray carpet ran tightly from wall to wall. It
was the color of static, and seemed as hateful. Molly was drunk.
Each month, as long as she believed she might be pregnant,
she couldn't drink. Drinking was an aspect of her—again—
defeat. A bed sealed in white chenille, sporting a frail iron
headboard, had been jammed against wallpaper adrift with
plushy roses. Bees scaled to those blooms would have been the
size of ping-pong balls. The only window overlooked the dark
street, empty except for David's little car. Molly smiled down
on it.

In a chipped sink, before a postcard of mirror, she washed
in water so icy it rang in the bones of her hands. Though David
was waiting downstairs with the grim old woman, and there
wasn't much time, Molly fell back on the bed. The ceiling

tipped one way, then the other way, righting itself beautifully. She had never even considered the chance that she might be unfaithful to Joe. Only the opposite. In this bed? It was like her *grandmother's*. Molly bit her hand to keep from laughing. Her grandmother's bed had been like this, exactly like it, down to the chenille spread, the tiny white cottontails Molly used to love picking at as she daydreamed her way through a fever. Molly's grandmother had lived with them. Molly had been put to bed in her grandmother's room with measles. This was done to keep Molly away from the little brother and sister she was sure to give measles to. Molly remembered the exhilarating warnings that she could go blind if she looked out the window, and the smell of her own body, sick, and the compulsiveness with which she'd picked and picked at the chenille. She was forbidden to read, and monotony was absolute, the shades drawn to the sills, old shades, that heavy old yellow parchment kind you never see anymore.

Getting up, she kissed the iron bedstead's post, kissed the knob on top, kissed her own goose-pimpling arms as she undressed; then into a dress that was suddenly not just an expensive but a *beautiful* dress. How could you know, buying a dress, whether it was beautiful or not? This was a mystery to which Molly had never been initiated, though women all around her understood it, assumed it was simple—your body, its virtues and drawbacks, the right dress. This was *luck*. Mascara for her lashes. Back in the chilly little bathroom again. Chap Stick, not sexy, necessary. She was taking too long. Terra-cotta powder, Aziza, to bring out her eyes' green. The mirror she stared into had a crack up its middle, so that one of her eyes was higher than the other. Molly was suddenly stone-cold sober and full of fear.

"Book, book," she called to her bags, sorting through. Instead of the book, she picked out the sheaf of new poems. To ensure that this was a decision, she latched her bag and got out of the room. At the head of the stairs Molly stopped, apprehensive about the steepness, the heels she wasn't good in, and from his horrible chair David mimed opening a book. She held up the folder; his eyebrows lifted. Her descent was self-conscious but fine. He was willing her to be fine.

"New poems," he said in his car. "I'm flattered."

"*You* are."

"We are." He said carefully, "You can't know: I haven't said: I love your work."

She told him, "Lately I've hated it."

"Hated it." A question.

"It seems so limited by *about*ness."

"Don't dislike it, it's a waste," he said, and seemed serious.

She told herself he was being good at his job, but still, she was pleased by him—his hand on the steering wheel, glanced over by light, the valleys between his knuckles, the specific veins.

She wanted him to keep driving, for them not to get there, but this wish ended in another parking lot, her face stung across by rain, unfresh, industrial-city rain, the folder under her coat. They were both conscious of David's not putting an arm around her as he ushered her up stone steps where people were standing around forlornly. These creatures dressed in black, almost to a man—because they were all men (boys)— had the air of having waited for some time, crying, "David! At last!" If David didn't feel guilty, she wasn't going to. He unlocked great double doors and led her down a hallway whose floor of varnished wood was rapidly tracked over by the trailing pack. David parted another, even grander pair of doors to peer into a dim auditorium, and she was struck with the worst fear yet: tiers and tiers of seats in bottle-green plush, their scrolled wooden arms braced by brass. Many of the seat backs had shadows worn in the plush where heads had lolled in boredom. Air released at last from a sarcophagus would be this intimidatingly dead. She couldn't do it. Molly chewed her lower lip for an animating taste of her own blood.

"You look a wee little bit worried."

Molly said, "I am a wee little bit."

"I can take care of you."

"You're paid to."

"I would anyway."

Taking her arm, he steered her fast down the hall, dodging two or three sodden idlers in black, who looked interested at being dodged. A closet of an office: from its disarray, she guessed it was his. On the wall, Auden presided, his forehead and fallen cheeks as rucked and rilled, as tragically complex, as cortex. Marianne Moore had taken refuge, her fastidiousness intact, disliking *it* and almost everyone, under an eave of black hat. Dylan Thomas, disenchanted, slipstreamed cigarette smoke. Books had fallen everywhere. Books covered even the solid black typewriter with its long-stemmed keys alertly uplifted. "No computer," Molly said. "No," he said. Molly let her fingertips fit into cold silver cups. She typed, setting books hopping and then thumping to the floor. DAVID was five pops and then a silence in which he came near to rub at her cheek. "Rain has melted something here," he said. "Under this eye. Come on, I'm not very good at this. You must help."

She scrambled through her purse. Handkerchief. She touched until he nodded. "You might brush your hair," he said critically. She sat down in his chair and did as she was told, surprised to find her hairbrush in the rubble of her purse, her hair snapping, Joe's earring slanting across her jaw as she tipped her head. Joe. She thought how she had conjured him at supper—shaping their house with her hands. "Let's try this," David said, sliding open a drawer. They drank a slow burn from a flat golden bottle. She wanted to open his other drawers to see what she could find. She wanted to read all the letters spilled over the desk to find out whether anyone loved him or he loved anyone or whether these were only the usual mutually flattering exchanges about who would come to read in that deathly auditorium. And what pittance they were to be paid and what train they should climb on to get here. He could not be on everyone's train, could he?

"I didn't ask *why* you were in London."

"We must go, Molly. Time. It really is."

"Why were you? Tell."

"A friend of mine is in hospital."

"Is he all right now?"

"She," he answered softly.

"So you have a friend," she said. Of course. How could someone like him not have a friend? "She's all right?"

"She's dying." He shook his head. "It's not getting any more real—dying, not possible, not her, no, but she is. *She* believes it."

"I'm so sorry."

"I know."

"Are you all right?"

"No, not all right, not for some time now, not all right, but fine." He stroked her hair away from her forehead: he made her a little girl and told the little girl, "Come on now. Read me some poems."

Molly was at the lectern, braced against it, newly introduced by David, newly abandoned by David, aware, before she began speaking, that her voice would be hoarse, suffering the dream moment—no book!—before she remembered she'd brought the sheaf of poems instead. Nine, no, a dozen, no, fourteen foreign faces in the tiered darkness, and *Molly* in a love poem,

Molly and Joe lying together, she resting with her chin on his chest, he caressing her naked back. What was wanted was a baby—the child they could evoke for each other, imagine, but maybe not cause to *be*. It struck Molly that she was confiding these confusions not to the—twenty-two? She'd miscounted, or latecomers had snuck in—heads out there, but privately to David. She turned the page, the microphone magnifying this to a giddy crack. The widely spaced, laggard clapping caught her off guard, already into the next poem, another love poem. Too late she understood she had picked up the folder on the spur of the moment so that she could expose the most intimate aspects of her existence to twenty-two contemptuous faces. Here was Joe again, and here was Molly lying naked along him, above him, her legs V'd to match his longer legs, remembering making snow angels when she was small. The poem ended with that month's disappointment. It was graphic enough. "Menstrual," in her new hoarse voice, rang around the dreary dimness, rousing a spindly young man who sat up and began coughing on a note of amazement. His coughing punched through a bronchial aria, faltered, accelerated to a frightening intensity. "Menstrual" had startled and was possibly going to kill him. His hacking extinguished itself in a snarl of nose-blowing. Molly dealt him, and this prolonged interruption, her all-purpose ironic *This could only happen to me* smile, which had saved a lot of bad moments, bad public moments, because the truth was nobody would blame the young man for really ruinous awkwardness, but only Molly. She could seem rueful, but not chastened; genuine embarrassment on her part would appall the room. She would have liked to be able to count on the next poem, but these were new poems and she had no idea what it was. She was a fool.

The dark wants something: to get darker.

Dark, then a more serious darkness, slid down the pages of Molly's book, and she was lost. She'd forgotten she was on a train—it seemed, now, a wonderful thing not to have known, but she needed to stop thinking about this afternoon in order to get through now, this poem, an early Joe poem, sex exclusive of the will to conceive, un-baby-haunted. *Molly* had been so bold as to fall in love at first sight. She envied *Molly,* and regretted everything that had gone wrong in real life since *Molly* fell in love, five years' flawed, because real, love. Her next book would be more complicated.

She said "Thank you" and was through.

"Wow," David said. He was holding her coat, and she backed toward him, sliding her arms down sleeves. He had been keeping track of what she needed—a kiss; the privacy in which to rue a kiss; reassurance; now her coat. Her coat was simple. "What do you mean, 'Wow'?" she asked over her shoulder, and was told, "You were great." She let herself be led out into the night, miserable at having to mistrust him for the first time. On the stone stairs, she found her book thrust at her, and signed it. Her book was unfamiliar, far from home. It had stopped raining. A dozen watchers, pale faces, dark scarves, apprehensive patience, were waiting, and David said, "Would you like to visit the pub?" She said, "Yeah, sure," and they laughed and echoed her, "Yeah, sure." Even walking back to his car she could hear it, once or twice more, "Yeah, sure," floating after her, and David unlocked his little car and they rattled down streets between reefs of absolutely uniform row houses, each with its bare stoop. One, two, three steps up to a narrow door was repeated infinitely throughout Cardiff. She had believed London bleak, but this city was far more impressive in the authority with which it ruled out any possible deviation from depression. In London there had been little relieving touches, a door sporting a lion's-head knocker, an old woman tenderly chiding her leashed Yorkies as they powered her along, the silent people waterfalling down the Underground's escalators. Here David was the only beautiful thing. The bar was a low-ceilinged room packed with grim

men in caps who shifted only slightly to let Molly and David
through. Men addressed one another over Molly's shoulders,
and when a pipe was rapped smartly against the wall behind
her, she jumped. David had deserted her; two young women
took his arms and dragged. He made a *wait there* face at Molly,
so she waited twenty dizzy smoky minutes, Welsh voices roar-
ing around her. *I'll go to sleep,* she thought, *right here on my feet,
and none of them will notice, and because we're all packed in so close
together I won't fall over.* She felt entirely safe among the men.
Maybe this was the right relation to men, to be crushed in
among them, involuntarily comforted by their bigness and
smokiness and tweediness, their almost roughness, but utterly
ignored, not *there* to them, as if you sat on your father's lap
and he forgot you. She yawned deliciously, with liberating
rudeness, then looked around to see who'd noticed. Of course
the poor hacker, in need of forgiveness, was there to notice.
Of course he came toward her hastily, carrying sturdy glasses
golden with whiskey. She drank, listening closely, hardly able
to follow his apology for his accent. She wished it were possible
to say *I forgive you I forgive you I forgive you* and have him vanish
back to the underworld, but it wasn't. He was compelled to
explain. The explanation compounded as no one else came for
her. He had suffered from this cold for two months now. What
did one do for colds in America? She told him she lived in the
northern New Mexico desert, which was where D. H. Lawrence
had been exiled for tuberculosis, hoping he would not take
this for an invitation to visit. He lived with his mother, he
told her, a formidable woman really, though confined to a bath
chair—bath chair?—and her twenty cats. Molly was sure she
had heard wrong but he insisted no, indeed, twenty cats; some
nights they all started howling at once. She knew she was
going to carry his hopeless bachelorhood, his narrow bed blan-
keted with the laziest and most intimidating of the cats, home
with her, and that she had lost David to the local girls who
loved him well before she, Molly, got here.

But no, here he was, David's hand on her shoulder to subtract her from her admirer, David telling the hacker, "I've got a great treat for your cats."

"My mum's cats. What is it, then?"

"I'll come by tomorrow." David betrayed the hacker, then, whispering in Molly's ear, "A great bore, eh?," finding her another whiskey, introducing her around to people he assured her she had to know.

It was forever before they were through with this. Back in his car, he set the wipers flogging at the rain. It was only by serious effort that she kept herself from leaning into him, resting her head on his shoulder. This seemed, vaguely, a bad idea, though the reason why proved elusive.

"I'm afraid I won't see you at all tomorrow," he said. "I'm away early. To London."

To his friend. Molly said, "I'll miss you."

He let it pass and she said, just as lightly, "Miss the chance to talk to you," because this was both true and a way of saving face. Couples choose so fast—*immediately*—which is the elusive one, and she'd understood since the train that in whatever haphazard, neither entirely *meant* nor *felt* fashion they were a couple, that the elusive partner was not her, married, American, going home tomorrow, but him. His life was more absorbing to him than hers was to her—a shameful truth she could qualify by adding, *for now.* She didn't want her life back yet, but wanted him, wanted this briefest of brief lives with him.

He was talking. "Impossible to believe in, at first. The usual response, right, but you find yourself evading reality, and you wonder, *What am I capable of? How far would I run?*, meanwhile doing what's necessary. Hating yourself, willing yourself through some phase of her dying, because there's only so much to her dying—it's finite, the process, yet you resent what you have to do, you're not grateful for these last things. Now it needs only a very small tilt and I'll be alone. I will do

all my thinking alone; she won't exist. Am I explaining at all
well?"

She didn't want to know what his friend was dying of,
though this wasn't like Molly, this willingness to leave it at
that, to let him tell her what he wished to tell her, to leave it
to him. "I wonder what—I can't think how to ask this, but
what it does to love, a love that already existed."

"You try to tell each other everything, before."

She couldn't answer.

"Now I wonder where she's going with what she knows.
What will happen to what she knows." He said, "Will it feel
as though it's all gone into the dark, or will I believe she still
knows what she knows," not a question. He said, "She is who
I told everything to," and waited.

She couldn't help.

He thought safer ground lay in getting back to her. "Is
there someone you tell everything?"

"My husband. Joe."

"You're lucky, then."

"He has a kid by his first marriage. I tell Alden a lot—
he's five, and I'm interested how to, uh, tell him the truth.
Beginner's truth, you know? Truth for five-year-olds." She was
scrambling, too.

"Are you cold?"

"No. This is nice."

At the door of her hotel she waited for David to lock
his car and follow her in. Her landlady had abandoned the
downstairs but left the silenced television on. Fans of wan light
opened and closed between the grim chair legs and along the
gracelessly arched back of the divan, or love seat, or whatever
it was. Molly wanted very badly to sit there with David, but
she let this wish flick open and closed without his observing
it—without, she hoped, his observing it. At the foot of the
stairs she listened; patiently, he explained she would be picked

up and driven to the train at eight by a friend of his, someone she'd met at the pub, someone she'd already forgotten, she confessed. No matter. She would be seen off. This was her last little piece of being taken care of; she hesitated to feel herself her own responsibility again. "You were very good to me," she said. "My job," he said. "Good night, then." "Good night." Nothing at all was left to keep them standing there. In her heels she risked a step. She was so tired. She turned around. She was above him, bending, her hair falling into his face. He was kissing her, locking his hands together in the small of her back so suddenly that her back cracked.

There was the concluding, minky, oblique brush of beard as he set his cheek to hers and rested with her like that. They were old friends who could do no wrong with each other, who were full of trust, who had made up every argument, who couldn't part. His breath stirred her hair. She felt it even inside her ear. He let her go. She was watched up the hatefully steep stairs, and when she shut her door behind her, she leaned against it, very still. She hadn't heard him walk away from the foot of the stairs, and it was possible to hear everything in that sleeping house. How quiet they would have had to be, making love. For some reason that struck her as a particularly painful thing to have given up, the silence they would have had to observe, making love. She would have been good at it, careful. She lay on her bed, thinking she wasn't going to sleep at all, letting first the left shoe fall away and then the right, sure she could tell when the house was emptier by him. She moved her head sideways so that she was no longer staring ceilingward but at the old window brimming with cold night. There was still time to run to the window, open it, lean out, call down into the dark street. After a long wait she heard his car start, backfiring. Her last chance evaporated down the street into Welsh silence. When she was sure he was gone she went barefoot across the prickling carpet to the window and shoved it shuddering upward. He would have heard her clearly. She leaned out, but there were no taillights burning at the street's far end, no last-minute change of heart. Two kisses: their entire story, and who was she to pity herself, to think *Molly Molly Molly you fool,* to *miss* him like this, bitterly?

All the steep little row houses were dark. She dropped her dress to the floor, and back on her bed she considered the ceiling with its square milk-glass fixture, within which could be detected the faint fallen pallor of a moth, several moths overlapping, pale against pale against the glass. The night assured her it was a sleepless night, just now making itself known. When she stirred on the bed, it was only to draw her legs up so that she could wedge her chin against a knee, fetally, holding her own ankles, making herself small. Does Joe know himself, at this moment, loved? Was this love, saying no to something that was, in its way, love? Molly talked to herself. She told herself she wasn't going to figure it out tonight. She told herself to sleep.

She didn't sleep, or not much. At breakfast, she was aware she appeared disheveled. Luckily, there was coffee, not only tea, at the table set about with indifferent boarders—indifferent, at least, to Molly—and she was on her third cup when the hacking admirer of the night before arrived to drive her to the station. He drank a rapid cup of tea, explaining: David's friend could not, at the last moment, get away, and had rung him up, and he was only too pleased to help out in a pinch.

He talked for both of them on the drive to the train station, and he pressed questions with a solicitous tilt of his head, not really taking his gaze from the road, so that she felt comforted by his interest, no longer repelled by his neediness. When she shook his hand, finally, his grip was knuckly, passionately courteous, memorable. "Do have a nice journey," and she was on the train, and she was on an airplane, sleeping, waking uneasily, sleeping again. Customs. Another flight, though shorter, to Albuquerque. The people on this flight began to look like her people—whether she liked them or not, hers, the harried mother dealing herself tarot cards while her two kids plucked futilely at her gauze sleeve and the baby patted the window between it and the dark; the huge, huge-bellied Santo Domingo man whose sleep, like a bear's, rendered the passengers on either side of him fearfully immobile; the young, very young, Spanish kid who flirted with the girl beside him by rolling up a shirtsleeve to show Christ on the cross. Molly slept. Waking, she oriented herself by the narrow shafts of light on innocent heads. For a time she had forgotten her real life; it was like forgetting she was on a train. Whatever she deserved, she was going to be fine. She was fine, she was on the ground, Joe towing a raft, an extravagance, of Mylar balloons toward her.

I want this, she thought, of him running, dodging in and out to get to her, *this life.* His urgency turned heads, caused little *Ohs,* earned the world's indulgence, unreliable but given to them, not them in particular but them as lovers, kissing, Joe breaking off the kiss to say, "Hey, I know you," and, again, "I know you," while what she could hear over and under what he kept saying was unreal—was applause.

Honey

Solidity, sober commitment, a roof over each dark Dominguez head—those are the things Mercedes desires for her children, desires with the erratic detachment from them illumining this, her sixty-third year. She did not bring seven children from Nicaragua in order for them to choose the doomed American existence of nerves rubbed raw by divorce, of quarrels, mutual contempt, and lawyers' costly ministrations, but their lives unravel in spite of her, coming undone even as she grows older, more secretly watchful, and

increasingly pained in her estimation of what they are wasting.
In the wavy mirror with which the airline has grudgingly
outfitted its ladies', Mercedes could be sixty-eight, her pinned
hair harshly white, or fifty-five, her pupils as pitch-black as when
her husband, long dead, found his tiny horseshoe-mustached
reflection there. Mercedes observes her eyes lovingly in the mirror
and discovers she can no longer summon up his face.

She was his life, he said, his heart, his dove, tendernesses
that, thus recollected, sting faintly as they pass through on
their way back to the cool black vault that holds her marriage,
her children's childhoods, and their life in Nicaragua. For an
instant, under unlocked Nicaraguan palms, a child rides her
shoulders, rubbing a leaf over Mercedes's forehead; another
child swings crying from her husband's hand, two more race
barefoot down the darkening dirt road before them. The fric-
tion of these details against Mercedes's composure is acute; far
worse is the shock of her gross, consummate infidelity in having
forgotten her husband's face. Her heart thuds alertly, fearfully
trying to take the measure of this event. This is the first form
grief takes with her—a sudden despair in standing still—and
because the dim stainless-steel wedge of a bathroom could not
be more confining, she turns stiffly around and around until
dizziness seats her politely on the closed lid of the toilet.
Someone knocks and goes away. The ache, which belongs to
her heart, abruptly descends to her stomach. Mercedes kneels
to vomit. The pilot, a voice from far away, announces they are
beginning the initial descent into Albuquerque, New Mexico,
where the temperature on the ground is ninety-nine degrees.
Mercedes scarcely has the will to wash, to repin her disheveled
hair, to neaten her clothes, before finding her seat between two
salesmen. On earth, she is met by someone ponderously tall,
absurdly red-haired, breathing wine into her face as he bends
to her, as he tastes her pitiless old cheekbone with a son-in-
law's kiss.

This son-in-law, burdened by her bags, blind to her mood, finds the chip of emerald that is his old BMW in the glittering midsummer parking lot. Mercedes feels herself begin to fear it, the desert. In the car's backseat, sheltered from the sun by the almost subsonic murmur of air-conditioning, is a boy, chin on his knees, eyes closed, Sony Walkman riding his ears. The boy has achieved the otherworldly privacy of a fetus, and is not about to acknowledge their arrival. Stranger still, the son-in-law offers no apology for his son's rudeness. Mercedes remembers him distinctly as a nice boy, too tall for his age, an elusive, embarrassed presence at his father's wedding to her daughter. Swinging out into swift late-afternoon traffic, the son-in-law runs through deferential Spanish phrases. He inquires whether she recalls his son from the wedding. Yes: Mercedes from her vantage point studied the boy sharply, believing him to be the chief obstacle to her daughter's happiness, but he had not seemed troubled by the marriage. He had known just where the ring was. He had been wearing it on his own little finger. A twist, and he offered it up, smiling. Mercedes's son-in-law wonders whether her flight was comfortable, hopes that she is not overtired, and assures her that her daughter will be insanely happy now that she is here at last.

Mercedes prefers to keep her distance from her children, her two sons and five daughters. In the domino theory of daughters, each, submissively tipping into domesticity, sets the next in motion. Only Caro resisted. Rumors of her love life filtered across the U.S.A. to the Brooklyn garret where Mercedes sews for her living, though none of her children like it that she lives alone. Anything could happen to her, they threaten. Seven children have taken turns at badgering or sweet-talking her out of Brooklyn. Her own vigilance, which made her more or less successful at protecting small, straying children, is irritating to Mercedes, now that it has been instilled in those very children. What Mercedes likes is settling each morning to her old Singer before her domain of roofs, of spires, of bare trees and tire swings. Summer is best, when the wind balms the nape of her neck, exposed by the pinned-up wiry wreck of her old hair, her cat sleeps on the windowsill, and the Brooklyn light falls lovingly on the cloth.

A lunar mountain range glides by on the right, steep points of bare stone, crevasses shadowed in powerful deathly blue. Her son-in-law wonders in English whether she is feeling the altitude. "It might make you sleepy," he says. The mountain range is replaced by a vast dun horizon in which there is no hope at all. "Why did you come, Kev, if you're not going to talk?" Hart asks. No answer, only the popping and sizzling of miniaturized rock and roll.

In the strange, rambling house, Mercedes follows the boy. Like his father, he is an American giant, burdened by her bags, constrained by her frailty. Already she is tired of making tall people uncomfortable. He runs through an explanation she can't follow, either because she's exhausted or because in his embarrassed adolescent way he talks too fast. Swinging around at a doorway, he says, "Sorry," and offers with transparently faked, kind-to-a-stranger patience, "I was only saying Caro's sleeping. She's never out of bed in the afternoon anymore."

Determined to convince him she's understood perfectly, Mercedes fixes her face into a trance of shrewd attentiveness, but the expression fails to convince him, because her elderly foreignness slides between them like a glass door.

Her beautiful daughter must have been eating like a pig. Her deep-set Dominguez eyelids have fattened, her small jaw is soft, and her belly is the moon. "Oh, Mama," Caro says, pushing up in bed. "You know what I want? I want you to braid my terrible hair." They touch cheeks; they kiss; this time it is a mother-and-daughter kiss, tolerance on one side, charming pleading on the other. Caro has always wanted some-

thing from her mother; what she wants varies, but invariably
she never quite gets it. Mercedes confronts her mass of hair,
warm because Caro's been sleeping in it. It is Mercedes's own
hair of thirty years before. Mercedes says, "A brush," is handed
one, and notices, as she begins with a particularly cruel snarl,
that her daughter's left ear, triply pierced and once adorned
with opals and gold, is naked, and therefore touchingly childlike again.

"I went to the doctor this morning, Mama."

"You did? So?"

"Nothing, *nada,* no dilation, no softening of the cervix.
No sign that I'm going into labor. Time is so long now,
Mama. A day is ten years."

At her wedding, Caro acquired not only her older husband
but that husband's son, complex relations with the husband's
Waspy ex-wife, and this house set remotely in the Rio Grande
gorge. At first it was the house—a straggle of dim adobe
rooms, very old—that puzzled Mercedes most. Dirt walls,
water bugs, and neighbors with goats—they had those in
Nicaragua. How to keep the grandchild from falling into the
river that breathes a reedy dankness right into the house when
a window's left up? Caro has no idea how children are.

"She said—"

"Who said?"

"Mama, the doctor said we might try making love. Sometimes sex gets labor going."

How children are: they scald their hands, and puffs of
blister as translucently unreal as jellyfish fill their palms. They
get stung, and howl. They stain themselves with food, muck,
blood, dust. In their bowel movements appear lost buttons and
snail shells. Rashes flourish on their thin arms and disappear
overnight. Storms of coughing begin at moonrise.

"But, Mama, it's been months since we made love.
Months."

In swift, habitual rhythm, Mercedes braids.

"I have to tell you what's wrong with Kevin, too." Caro glances over her shoulder to stop her mother's hands. Caro says, "A girl he liked killed herself five months ago. She swallowed a bottle of her mother's prescription pills."

Mercedes touches forehead, heart, shoulder, shoulder. "Her poor mother," Mercedes says. "Her poor father."

"Her father wasn't there."

"And why not?"

"Mama, that's irrelevant. They were divorced a long time ago. Kevin didn't even know this girl long enough to love her."

"He says that?"

"He says he loves her. How would he know? Does he have to wreck his own life now, is that love?" Caro sighs. "Hart and I try, but no one can reason with him. It will take time, we say, and he shrugs as if he hates us. He seems so far away from all our little concerns. I love him, you know. I keep trying to draw him back in."

"And?"

"Nothing works. Nothing. He's making his father crazy." Caro yawns. "And, Mama, I'm selfish enough to wish they weren't all I was thinking about right now. The baby has only this little leftover piece of my attention. Look." She tosses *Your Baby and Child* at the closet, jammed with the winsome thrift-shop dresses the unpregnant Caro fancied. "I wanted to start there," Caro says. There is a crib in the corner, but it isn't made up. The exposed mattress ticking bothers Mercedes, as does the decal of a dancing bear, one of its paws torn off. "I thought I'd get the nesting instinct," Caro says, "and instead I'm the Blob." Mercedes counts dirty teacups on the dresser. She had expected Caro's house to be cleaner, and finds herself disapproving. The disapproval is a mother's, nimbly inserting itself into a welter of other, more reasonable emotions, where it will be hard to weed out.

"Lie down. Put your head in my lap," Mercedes instructs. A pregnant daughter calls on her mother for solidity, reassurance, proof that her fears are thin as air, and will vanish at the first maternal reproof. Caro sleeps. Mercedes has her work cut out for her. This room, then the rest of the house. What is needed here is not only Mercedes's brand of astringent housekeeping but a makeshift serenity. A harmony sufficient for a baby to be born into. The old sensation of being hemmed in by need sweeps over Mercedes. Today she has come three thousand miles. She arches her tired back, and doubles an elastic band around the end of Caro's braid. On the messy bed in the sad room, Mercedes begins to shake her head, slowly at first, anxiously, tiredly, then stops. Stops to wonder what she thinks she is doing here, and how she found the strength to stay away so long.

This old woman with the quaintly strained English, her dry cheeks collapsed inward below cheekbones that bleakly suggest the skull, her still-dark eyes critically aglitter, causes Hart to feel himself a lurching monster in his own house. He rests his Frankenstein forehead in his huge white-male hands and appeals for help, for something to save him from this plate of black beans, rice, and *huevos,* two doilies of fried egg slopped from the spatula onto his plate as his wife's belly bumps the back of his chair. *Consider your secretiveness,* Phil Donahue says, far back in Hart's brain. *Has he been drinking already this morning, can anyone in this audience tell?* The old woman wields her flatware with an immigrant daintiness. She's here to save her daughter, that much is unmistakable. Black beans and rice mean home to Mercedes: her daughter is dishing up Nicaragua, where they gossiped endlessly without the benefit of U.S. Sprint, where they cooked up steaming messes of beans and rejoiced in the reign of the father.

Breakfast, for Kevin, is a cup of loganberry yogurt. He is so silent Caro does not argue with him about eggs. He can stand his father, stepmother, and Doña Mercedes only as long as it takes to consume three hundred calories. He is six feet tall.

Kevin's mother, Hannah, is away now, gone to Europe with her boyfriend, Florian, a doctor who has his own house on a canal in Amsterdam. A modest house, but filled with aqueous shimmer, with goose-down duvets, mirrors, antiques, and a bathroom with bidet, heaven for Hannah, whose home has no bathroom at all. She has been poor ever since the divorce, maliciously, flauntingly penniless, with a poverty she can throw in Hart's face. She sold their big suburban place after the divorce to buy, near El Rito, a ruin needing everything: floors sanded down, roof insulation laid in, windows double-glazed against the northern New Mexico winters. In short, a fortune vanished there. The house was a black hole, but Hannah will never divorce it, and Kevin, cutting kindling, lugging a chain saw out through biting wind to the woodpile, latching the outhouse door against the vast nights, grew up fast. In that house, alone with Hannah, he had responsibilities, and they did him no harm.

Of course Kevin led another, parallel life, as children of dissolved marriages do. Hart went through a series of viewless condos and cheap apartments. Into each of these, one after the other, Kevin helped him move. Hart would boil up two of those frozen dinners that came in pouches, then tip the steaming water, with its pale plasticky smell, into cups for instant coffee. He was troubled by insomnia, the worst of his life, and he fell in love every other month, and was bewildered when an ex-lover came knocking on his door, or ranted at him over the phone. Living long weekends with Hart, Kevin learned roughly a thousand times more about him than Hart ever knew about his own father. Moreover, Kevin seemed infatuated with an existence in which he could be the ordering force. He slid

Roach Motels behind the grimy stoves, he dyed the water in
the toilets azure. He scoured the sinks, he read letters left
lying around, he knew and forgave everything, at least until
the unexpected happened: his father and his mother began
going out together. Parties, galleries. Oh, they were careful
with each other, and very careful to be sure that Kev's hopes
were not aroused. Hart came in so very, very softly from those
dates that, one night, he overheard "You love each other, you
love each other" recited by Kevin, belly-down in his soiled
sleeping bag, the door of his room half open. But Hart and
Hannah failed again in slow motion, because sometime in the
middle of this, Hart met Caro.

Kevin swigs coffee. "Not so fast," Hart says, surprised to
find himself talking in Phil Donahue's paternal tone, and is
countered by his son's silence, the slender, nervous gliding of
bolts into place.

Kevin met Katie at a party on their lawn alongside the
river last spring, when the Rio Grande had a glassy green,
rising smoothness from snowmelt, and the guests were all
pleasantly sweated up from working on the fence on the slope.
Among the hammering, nailing grown-ups was a girl. A
mare's tail of fine dark hair clung to her baby-oiled back, and
when she turned to stare at somebody over her shoulder, a line
of new tenpenny nails glittered in her clenched mouth. Hart
has thought back to it again and again, that girl with the
indifferently beautiful back turning to reveal her sea-urchin
mouth.

She was looking at Kevin for the first time. At Kevin
whose dark head is bent tediously over yogurt. Hart asks,
"Have you gone through that blue book yet?"

"What?"

"You were supposed to check those used-car prices, so that
when we went looking you'd know what was a fair offer. You
said you'd take an active part in this."

"Hart." Caro intervenes so softly it stops him. Too late.

"I will. I'm going to." But Kevin's tone is defensive, and Hart guesses he can be no help to anyone on anything yet, but it would be a good thing if he had a car. They're so isolated, out here in the gorge. They're about to disappear into baby world, leaving Kevin behind, on his own. On his slender own.

"I expect you to do what you tell me you'll do," Hart says.

Kevin swears, rattling Doña Mercedes, who draws herself up, frigid Catholicism in a housedress.

Hart, who has never had much room for anyone else's disapproval of Kevin, jumps into decisiveness. "We'll go this afternoon anyway, all right? Want to, Kev?"

"Not today," Caro says. "Not now." *"Now"* rhymes with *"miaow,"* it's so plaintive.

Is it doing Caro any good, having her mother here? At night, Caro seizes Hart's shoulder or tugs at his hair; grinding his molars together to stifle his yawn, eyes slitted, he rolls over, he asks her tenderly, "What?" and she tells him. She dreamed she was about to give birth in a strange, dirty swimming pool. She was going into labor in the stall of a public restroom, graffiti spangling its walls, "FUCK YOU" and "FUCK ME" and the telephone numbers. Or the baby was born and she'd lost it. This last dream was particularly vulnerable to transmutation. She'd lost the baby in Safeway, she'd lost the baby in the hospital, or she'd left the baby sleeping on the lawn and it rolled into the river. After any of these nightmares, she is slow to be consoled. A back rub, a cup of tea, another quilt added to her heap, and she cries in his arms before sealing herself back into sleep, leaving him awake to prowl the house, studying the black, child-eating river through the living room's plate glass.

"I won't know where to find you," Caro says, "if you're wandering all over Santa Fe."

"Your mother is here," Hart says. The old woman gleams his way, dispatching her coffee. Caro travels light-footedly to the pot. Odd, for all her bulk, that she is still so prettily swift in anticipating her mama's wish. Mercedes pats the arm that pours the coffee, and Hart sees what he sometimes doubts: that they are, they clearly are, mother and daughter.

"Maybe you should go." Reversing herself, Caro grows cheerful. "Maybe your being gone will bring it on. A watched pot."

"I'll call in the middle of the afternoon," Hart promises.

The daughter bends for a hairpin and deftly drives it into the old woman's knot of white horsehair without again acknowledging her husband's existence.

One after the other, the cars they search out are junk. Blasted Chevys, battered Volkswagen Beetles well into their second or third mechanical reincarnations. All morning and well into afternoon, the only car Kevin likes is a brutalized MG with a bumper sticker reading HUG A VET. The vet is Monroe, idly tossing Oreos to his rottweiler while he explains that though he has led a long and happy life with the car, he could be persuaded to part with it now for seven hundred and fifty dollars. "What a crock," Hart says, over cheesecake at Denny's. Kevin argues hard. He's mechanical, and anyway he has a friend who works on foreign cars and owns all the wrenches. The MG is cool.

"No," Hart says, but the MG appeals to him as a car for Kevin. Its pleasingly seedy interior, so small that a girl (What girl? When will Kevin risk another girl?) would have to ride knee to knee with the driver, its quality of scraped daredeviltry so great for a first car. So infinitely desirable. "It'll cost a fortune in parts."

"I can take care of it. I will." Kevin's fingers alight on his breastbone—a vow, an unconscious one. Wow, Hart thinks, happy at this eagerness, which could not be more genuine. For once, possibly for the first time, Kevin has forgotten Katie Dubov.

"You'd have to."

"So, let me show you."

"So, let me think about it."

"I had an offer this morning," Monroe says when they swing by for a parting look. "It might still come through. I can't guarantee you this car will still be here when you get around to making up your minds."

"Let's go for it," Kevin pleads.

"That's not the way to make a major purchase, honey, under pressure," Hart says, and the magic of covetousness dies from his son's face. Hart has slipped and called Kevin "honey" in front of this earringed vet with his mean dog careening around his bare yard and his afternoon's beer cans lined up on the MG's hood, and something of the car's promise, the small-scale imported machismo it holds out to Kevin, dims.

Therefore, and probably predictably, Hart grows anxious to have the car. A subtle current of remorse, Hart's toward Kevin, runs just underneath the surface of the transaction, which Monroe senses and would exploit if he did not feel sorry for Kevin.

Kevin twists the key, and the MG startles into rattletrap authority. This is the thrill Hart has sabotaged for his son: Kevin's pleasure is partly, mostly, faked, and rings false. Hart says, "I'll follow you," and does, taking from his glove compartment a Spice Islands jar that once held—he sniffs—nutmeg. He drinks Johnnie Walker Black and tries to remember what newborns are like. They can't hold up their heads, he thinks, and when they mew, you wrap them tightly in a blanket so that only their faces show, making little Taos Indians of them. He thinks he remembers Kevin that way. How could that girl bear to kill herself? The MG's canvas roof is up. It is evidence of Kevin's tense, imperfect bliss that he did not at once wrench the roof down for this first drive. Black exhaust smokes from the MG's tailpipe on a long curve, and the father's heart goes *guilty, guilty, guilty,* all the way home.

Caro comes up the slope, her belly leading, her flip-flops clapping. The MG is exposed in all its failings. Its dented fender, its dappling of rust. Its broken headlight, crackled white quartz in chrome. Caro's disbelief, hidden by her sunglasses, finds a gesture: the flat of a hand set in the deep saddle of her back, her back arching more deeply, her belly jutting more extravagantly. "How much?"

"Seven hundred and fifty. What do you think?"

"Do I think we have seven hundred and fifty?"

"Would I have bought the car otherwise?"

"You don't agree you're sometimes impulsive?"

"No matter what it cost, you would have implied 'Too much,' Caro, wouldn't you? Anyway, it's too late now. It's done."

"He'll take it back."

"You don't know this guy."

"He'll take it back," she repeats. "The stupid, senseless greedy who sold it to you, you'll make him take it, you'll tell him it's not what you want after all. It's not safe. It's already been wrecked once, hasn't it?"

"Don't," Kevin says.

"Kevin is a good, reliable driver. You have to—"

"How can you yell?" Kevin says. "She's pregnant. How can you stand there and yell at her? If she hates the car, I don't like it either. I don't want it. I could see you thinking it would do me good."

Caro turns dark sunglass lenses his way. "Would it?" she asks. "Help?"

"Right. Would it help for me to have a car you hate? Right."

"If I stopped hating it?"

"If you stopped hating it, you'd be lying."

"If it was something you wanted, I wouldn't hate it. I'd stop."

"Because you think it would make me better."

"Because nothing else seems—"

"You think a *car* could do that?"

"Kev," his father warns.

"It's not going to be a car," Kevin says.

"I can see that," Hart says. "Then what?"

"It's not going to be you," Kevin says. "Not a swine like you." He looks at Caro. "And it's not you. I don't know you."

She protests, "You know me."

"Kevin, you stop," Hart says.

"You love my father who left my mother when she did fucking nothing to deserve it. You don't know how good she is. I don't have any idea why you married someone like him. I don't have any idea why you're having this baby."

Caro says, "Ow," her expression a delicate mix: alarm, satisfaction, wistfulness, fear. "It doesn't hurt," she says, marveling downward so that her sunglasses slide to the end of her long, upturned nose. "It feels like a little ribbon rippling around, like a drawstring getting drawn in."

"It's my fault," Kevin says.

"So what?" Caro says. "This is a fine time."

"You think everything in the world is your fault," Hart says to Kevin, and to Caro, "You're supposed to walk."

"To walk? Walk where?"

"Down the road. To encourage the contractions. Come on."

"Come too, Kev? Keep me company?"

He won't. "I don't want to be here."

Hart takes her elbow. "Another little pain's coming girdling around," she says. "Ow. It's nice. Ow. If my mother wasn't here, nothing would have been done in time, would it? The baby's bed would never have been made. Do you think she's cooking dinner?"

"Walk," Hart tells her.

Kevin runs down the slope. The screen door's single bark

rides up the hot air toward them, and Caro asks, "Why did he run?"

"To boil water," Hart says.

They walk down the dirt road, Caro swatting early mosquitoes from her bare arms, her gait wary and majestic. "Nothing else," she says, and ten minutes later adds, "It's not happening." She's still wearing her sunglasses, but her mouth, when she turns her face up, is stricken.

"Hey, so we go eat Mercedes's dinner," Hart says. "It's not the end of the world."

"Don't you want this baby?" Caro asks. And clop-clops away from him through hard sunlight, full of hurt. She would run if she could.

"We won't let you go on too long after your due date, no," Dr. Mendez says.

Caro asks, sounding anxious, "You don't induce labor, do you?"

"When the baby is two weeks late, the placenta is aging, and may no longer be supporting the baby well, and, yes, we sometimes do induce labor. First we'd run some tests to determine whether the baby is under stress—"

"Then Pitocin," Hart says.

"Then Pitocin, possibly, yes," the doctor says. She smiles from Caro to Hart, who is visibly anxious too, and asks, "Did you try my suggestion?"

They both glance guiltily away.

Hannah's Dutch boyfriend, Florian, has a head of curly hair and a libertine's merry eyes. He has, in addition, a quality of possessing great personal freedom in his relations with women. He is simply very clever with women; he knows how to catch them up immediately into conversation, a kind of conversation that another man would find repellent, almost viciously competitive—Florian presenting himself and his virtues—but often enough, women respond to this approach delightedly, indulgently, coquettishly. Sexually. Women love Florian. He wandered into a bookstore in Santa Fe and captured Hannah, who had been slouching against a wall under a bad but beautifully framed print, abstractedly rubbing strands of her own hair between thumb and forefinger, estimating their loss of silkiness, the onslaught of her own middle age, the probability that she would never have another child, her positively oppressive sense that she should at last read *The Mill on the Floss,* she should devote herself to that fat paperback for a hundred nights under her electric blanket although *Great Expectations* looked like more fun. Spendthrift that she was, she could afford both, and just as she was about to throw herself into the arms of the Victorians, there was cool Florian, his sexually forthright city as far from dampened England as it was possible to get in Europe, his eyes wondering just who *she* was, evaluating and elevating her, because there had been in Hannah's recent life such a dearth of male attention of any kind, shape, or form—except for that of her son and her ex-husband, of course; how could they count?—that finding herself read as a sexual creature caused her to unslouch herself, shake her fair head, and let her eyes focus on this interested foreign face. Here was Florian, full of promise. He'd come for her. Both knew it. It wasn't long before they disappeared together.

Now, whatever has happened between the divorced husband and wife, and almost everything has, she has never before left Hart behind. Hart knows about Florian because Hannah has always confided in him. Her confiding in him is a symptom of the fact that from the world of men who approached her, Hannah had chosen Hart for herself, and remained assiduously true to her choice well after they were divorced, suffering rather lightly the inevitable desertion of one fleeting boyfriend, a carpenter she had taken on more passively than passionately. Or so it seemed to her ex-husband. Since the carpenter, who left last year, the one and only man Hannah has slept with is Hart. Their lovemaking was an act so baldly needy and spontaneous, so short, unadorned, and potentially devastating, that Hart can't bring himself to weigh its meaning. Oddly, it appeared to mean more to him than to Hannah. What right has Hannah to flaunt her new equilibrium in his face? She was once sure she could not live without him. No longer. She doesn't even like him, she told him in bed. An amazing, cold, unexpected remark. It hurt and stirred him. In bed with her he had felt the change begin, a subtle thing and small, dwarfed by the bitterness in her voice when she repeated, "I don't like you. I don't like the things you do." The change, pitted from the first against skepticism harsh as Hannah's, had nonetheless begun there, in Hannah's bed, under Hannah's quilts, with Hannah's electric heater purring away at the sole of the single lovely, high-arched foot she aimed at it, with roughly the same degree of unself-consciously sensual practicality with which she had, five minutes before, shoved her pelvis upward to receive him more deeply. More satisfactorily. She had managed that for herself, though she no longer loved him.

Worse, as he soon came to realize, she was ashamed of having slept with him. As she came and went, dropping off or retrieving their son, Hart kept getting whiffs of her shame. Caro, five months pregnant, had begun to show. Hannah's shame smelled like a child's dirty hair, a sodden diaper, a cast about to come off a broken arm—some soiled, infinitely intimate thing.

This was the situation Florian stole her from. Hart, who can't blame her for going, can't forgive Hannah, either, for causing him to feel as if he has just, freshly, lost her; as if it were not he who had brought about their divorce, but her whimsical infatuation with Florian that tore apart some old, honest, married love.

When really Hart's only honest, relatively sane love is for Caro. Until she got pregnant she was, in bed, rich felicity, his great good luck. Pregnancy made her queer and touchy; her tongue flew through astounding recriminations even as her body receded from him to the pearly white, indifferent shore of late pregnancy. The fetus defeated its father, or at least its father's desire. It was, in Hart's experience, an unprecedented thing for desire to do—simply to leave him as easily as it had come—but once it was gone, he settled himself in to play expectant husband. He could believe himself happy among the squatting and blowing couples of their natural-childbirth class. He could time a pretend contraction with the best of them, and never avert his eyes from the film when the baby's head, surfacing like the glossily dark pit of a halved avocado, crowned in the huge vagina.

He pads barefoot into the cold kitchen. Mercedes has tidied it until it reflects the stasis of—of Heaven, he supposes, or possibly of her Brooklyn garret, sanctified by widowhood. He throws open the refrigerator door. His scrotum contracts in brilliant Arctic air, his heart aches, and he smells old bologna. He makes himself a huge, comforting feast of a sandwich, like a cartoon husband comically unaware of his place in the world—his humiliatingly small niche gazed into by huge, decisive women as they pass. Well, hello, telephone. The receiver's poison-control-center sticker, skull and crossbones, glows in the dark. Hart remembers the way that, in Hannah's warm bed, he felt the brisk angel's wing of his future pass over his heart. What had he wanted, how had he judged his chances, at that instant, her heater purring, the points of her collarbone flaring in her flattish, freckled chest when she threw her head back into the pillow, when she came? There is the telephone. Her number is on a slip of paper held with a magnet to their refrigerator. Like it or not, here it is, his new life: his ex-wife's number on the refrigerator among the coupons for Pampers, the Polaroids of friends' kids, the pre-divorce, pre-distrust picture of Kevin, then smaller and more radiant, crowned by a soccer ball, crowing with triumph, sun pouring down on him, on the green field he spent his eleventh summer on. Caro's eternal unfinished shopping list that reads *Skim milk, chicken breasts, toilet paper.* As far as he knows never a day passes when his household does not need chicken breasts. Caro is ready for this baby. Is he? He examines himself with an intensity that eats away a great rust of habitual, second-nature self-deceit and finds that, no, astonishingly, no, assuredly, *no,* he's not ready for this baby. He wades through the muck of this *no,* this terrifying black *no* nothing in him rises up to refute, to the telephone, and taps out the digits that will fly his voice toward a satellite, ricochet it off spacy cold metal to Europe, to that decaying old sea city where she is. *She answers on the second ring.* His surprise is minor, given the event.

But then again, so is hers. "You don't sound good," she says. "Let me sit up so I can think. There. I'm sitting." Then she recollects the terms they parted on. "What do you want? Is it Kev?"

"Nothing's wrong with Kev. This is me."

She's silent. "Hannah," he says.

"Yes. I said, *yes,* here I am, you found me. I'm hanging up."

"No, Hannah, no, it's this baby. I don't want this baby. I'm not ready."

She laughs.

"Hannah, don't laugh. I don't want it."

"Then you *are* in trouble," she says with a lilt, her voice not as unkind as her words.

"Don't tell me that."

"Don't tell you that? When anyone can see it? I'm going now."

"Hannah. Say you won't go until I'm all right."

"I can't do that," she says.

"Please."

Hart turns, hearing a sound. Behind him in the darkened kitchen, gazing at him with merciless, timeless recognition, is his mother-in-law. His mother-in-law has just heard him beg, despairingly, in the dark kitchen, *"Please."*

He swipes a dish towel from the counter and hangs it in front of his genitals. He says very clearly, "I'm not a bad man. Not as bad as you think."

Hannah says distantly, into his ear, "Try A.A., Hart."

Mercedes says nothing at all.

He fidgets the dish towel until his genitals are completely sheltered. How long does she mean to stand there? He says, "I can change."

Hannah says distantly, into his ear, "Good-bye."

Mercedes says nothing at all.

It leaves him nothing to go on, no clue about what will happen, the silence in which Mercedes sweeps from the kitchen.

In the small bathroom, in a dimness that seems to her unnatural—no lights outside the window; sounds, but no lights—Mercedes undresses down to the nitroglycerin patch she donned two hours ago against proof of her son-in-law's infidelity. It had been, for Mercedes, a scene of great violence, the big man with the dish towel hanging before him; the woman, whoever she was, who is so shameless as to fool with the husband of a hugely pregnant woman, to quarrel with him over the telephone in his own home in the middle of the night. In the middle of the night when such things should have been long ago settled, and the husband and wife in bed together.

Of course, Mercedes reflects, her own husband sometimes left their bed at just such an hour. Of course he went catting around, dishonoring their life together and all she was. His infidelity, great secret that it was, still pains Mercedes, two decades later and thousands of miles away, as she is an old woman meticulously flossing her long, elegant yellow teeth. He was unfaithful, and it was love between him and Mercedes. Though he was unfaithful, it was love and it remained love. Once or twice when he'd left the bed, she'd been no less pregnant than her besotted daughter is now. The difference between Caro and Mercedes is that she, Mercedes, will never see her husband's face again. No one exists to come back to bed. In her garret there are pictures, of course, but none of them are precisely the face she wants. The long, gallant salt-and-pepper mustache, the wide wings of the aggressive nose, the cobble of chin, the bright lover's eyes, had not photographed well. They are inexact as memory never was. Seizing the nitroglycerin patch by its corner, Mercedes peels it away. It leaves a small chemically scorched rectangle, pink as sunburn, over her heart.

He said, "I'm not a bad man," and though that was a baffling thing for him to assert under the circumstances, there is something in it Mercedes can't dismiss. When he said "I can change," it was, and she knows it was, the truth, and so they will go on together, her daughter and this palely alien American, and their life together will baffle Mercedes, surely, whatever else she learns about it, just the way her life would baffle them—or, for that matter, any of her children—if she ever chose to tell them anything about it. But really it was none of their business, how you lived. It was their business that you took care of them, that you were there to nurse them through fevers and catch them before they fell into the river, but what, apart from love like that, did they need? The truth is that she is almost done with them.

In her robe she stares down the hallway to the opening window, and finds Kevin climbing clumsily in. To Mercedes's surprise, he is naked except for drenched cutoff jeans. This must be her night for coming across hugely tall, nearly naked Anglos. He is as astonished to see her as she is to see him. He could not have expected from her such a torrent of hair, or such self-possession.

"I'm sorry," he says, crouching over the window. "You heard something, and were frightened."

"Do I look frightened? Is this the way you come into the house?"

"I am sorry," he says, and then, as if she were not standing there, he rakes his hand down his side, his long boyish bare rib cage, and Mercedes, coming closer, sees the rising dappling of hundreds of mosquito bites. He goes for them feverishly with bitten fingernails, so harsh with himself she can hear the scratching. She says, "You'll bleed." "I can't help it." "Stop that," she commands, but his is the impotent impatience of someone whose skin is *itching,* and despite his evident wish to appear polite to her, he can't stop. She reaches forward and seizes his wrist, which has a compact, knit-together solidity that feels adult and male, as does his reluctance to yield to her, but she is a general of little emergencies. "My room," she directs, and once there daubs his spots with oil of camphor from a neat brown bottle as he sits on the edge of her bed, leaning forward, his huge elbows on his big knees, his entire attitude a fusion of miserable courtesy and real relief. Through the tonic vapor of camphor she smells cold water drying from a child's skin. "You were in the river," she accuses his back.

Embarrassment freezes him.

"I could never have gone into a river," she tells his back. At his nape, his hair is drying in a curl. "No matter what I felt, I could never have gone into a river."

"It's our river," he says, and shudders when she touches his back again.

"You mean you're used to it."

"The way you're used to the subway, and the gangs."

"I do not court death," she says.

"Because to you, it's a sin."

"To you, it's not?" she asks, her voice going provocatively rueful. "And your father, and my daughter who loves you now, and the little brother or sister who is coming? You go into the water thinking of what they'll feel?"

His resentment is intact again. It lies in the millimetric tensing of his cold white back, and in the texture of his skin, which shifts in that instant from a grateful to a guarded passivity, so that she stops her doctoring and waits until he says, "I do think of them."

"You don't think of them enough, then. Imagine a vast hurt."

She gives him a moment to imagine it.

"Imagine them feeling it."

She gives him another moment.

"You would cause them such pain."

The expanse of his bare back, with its fine muscles, its rather daintily set shoulder blades, and the long channel, deeply indented, of the spine, waits on her.

She says, "You can't do that to them."

She says, "It's simply a thing you can't do."

She says, tipping the bottle into cotton, fitting cotton to a welt, "You're through with this now?"

He says, "I just want to stop feeling what I feel."

She takes a deep breath. She inhales hugely, as against some formidable physical task. She apologizes to her dead husband's beautiful forgotten face for the calm with which she is about to tell this truth. She says, "You will."

When Hart rolls over, he is as quiet as can be, but it's no use. He dislodges Caro from sleep. Her curly long hair lies in a mess on the pillow. When she turns toward him, he tries to take his bearings from her expression. "I had a good dream," she says. "I was riding my mother's shoulders down this dirt road, and it was going dark, and I was rubbing a leaf across her forehead, I don't know why."

"Why was that a good dream?"

"I had some idea the leaf was magic. That it could keep us all safe."

"You know what I wish?" Hart says. "I wish that damn girl had listened for her mother's key in the lock before she started swallowing."

"No one could have expected there to be a traffic jam that evening," Caro says.

He tries to settle into a position that is both companionable and will still allow for the possibility of sleep, but she sits up tailor-fashion and begins caressing her belly.

"Anything?" Hart says.

"Not a thing."

"You and your body," he says. "Don't you think you're as stubborn as your mother? Let me ask you something."

"Ask."

"What is it? Why hasn't she ever liked me?"

"She likes you." He looks at her, arching his eyebrows morosely. "My mother," she says. "My mother is a mystery. All the time when we were children, living together in the tiniest house"—she fixes him with a dark, judicious, almost accusing gaze—"in intimacy you can't even begin to imagine, each of us knowing every single thing about all the others, we still knew she was a mystery. I don't think you can change her mind about you, Hart. But it doesn't matter to me, what she thinks."

What will happen now?, Hart wonders, resting his knuckles on her defiant belly, pretending to knock, saying softly, "Come out, come out, and I'll be good to you," and she laughs and falls carefully onto her side in the rumpled sheets, the quilt sliding silently from the bed, she bringing her knees up and giving him a quarter-profile glance, and he locks a long arm around her, above her belly, under her breasts, and enters her from behind, and their pleasure in each other is so acute they forget it is meant to bring on pain.

Get It Back for Me

That night's argument was about love, because it was almost always love, because they couldn't exhaust the momentum of *If you loved me, then* and *You can't understand, because.* Dinner began when my father, sitting down to give the familiar left-right yank to his tie— chin dodging right-left, knot loosening—said ruefully, "At last." My mother dished mashed potatoes and wondered, "Is that an apology?" " 'Apology.' For?" "Are you saying you couldn't have gotten home sooner if you'd wanted to?" My

brother and sister in high chairs kicked and crooned and ate
from their own hands. A baby spoon fell. A comet's tail of
apricot kicked away from the spoon when it hit. Resentment was the light in my mother's eyes. My mother and father
were *at each other's throats:* out of nowhere, that evening, came
the phrase. I looked, foolishly spellbound by the words'
wolfishness, by their suggestion of actual red injury, at my
vivid mother. Her cardigan was unbuttoned two buttons down
on a nakedness whose collarbones were lucidly, almost freak-
ishly, *bones*. The hollow between them was deep, tensely set
off by tendons, deep, tense, quiet, quiet, quiet, then stroked
across by her pulse. I was never going to love any constellation
as I loved the array of pale-pink and dark, distinct moles visible
when this sweater was unbuttoned two buttons down. That
configuration of moles was the essence of my mother—it was
like a signal her body sent to the surface from unbelievably
deep, more *her* than her name, "Gracie" or "Mom" or "Ma-
ma-ma-ma-ma" according to who wanted her. She and I con-
spired so that I didn't want her often. She didn't like "Mom."
"Mom?" and her eyes began to think of something else. Con-
ceivably, she hated the word. Certainly it didn't do what it
was meant to—it failed to fix her attention entirely on me. It
didn't cause her to renounce all else. I could only agree with
her that "Mom" wasn't to be trusted. I trusted those moles
because they were serious and pretty and eternal. They appeared when buttons were unbuttoned. Undo this button,
undo the next—they had to appear.

My mother was waiting for an answer. My father's throat
was less exposed, his shirt buttoned to its collar button, his
tie still tied, though loosened and crooked. What showed in
his throat was the black-grained blush of the beard that wanted
to be there. It surfaced in the evenings, rudely male. His good-
night kiss could burn a cheek. His shirt was very white and
had the strictly ironed neatness she sent him out into the world
with. He had rolled up his sleeves.

The mashed potatoes had dried in peaks, and the roast beef was both gray and, depressed with a fork, bleeding. Shining small peas each contained a glint of unthawed, original cold as brilliant and brief-lived as a snowflake's. How she managed this, he said, was beyond him. Half the food cooked to death, half the food raw. She knew he was coming home. All she had to do, *all she had to do* was have dinner ready. His answer to her: One night, one night he'd like to come home to some kind of order. One night, one *night* of his *life* he'd like his wife to be happy to see him. The other guys' wives were happy when they walked in the door. She said, How did he know anyone else was so happy? How did *he* know? He wasn't walking in their doors, he was walking in this door, and all he could really talk about was *this* life, and he said they had to be happier than this, *had* to be.

Two hours later, when he began to take apart the pipe her ring had vanished down, my mother said neutrally, "Your shirt." His face, withdrawn from the cupboard's shadow, warned he hated to be interrupted. "My shirt?" "Will get stained. Greasy." The doors of the cupboard under the kitchen sink were open to reveal the silver, lightly sweating, cold undulation of pipe, a compressed horizontal S, its supporting leg disappearing through a crude hole in unpainted plywood. In the S's first tight horseshoe the ring was trapped, if it was trapped. My father had wondered aloud whether it had washed all the way through, in which case, he said, it was gone. He was impatient to find out. Small-scale problems that could go one way or the other, sharply *yes* or sharply *no*, tended to obsess him.

I sat cross-legged near his left foot, my attention not on him or on my mother but on the irregularity with which his slight duckfootedness, relic of childhood polio, had sanded down the heel of his shoe. When he was small (I knew the story), my father had spent a year in bed—hand-washed quilts, iron-bar bedstead, wallpaper sprigs and roses that would recur in his dreams for the rest of his life whenever he was sick. His mother, sure he was going to die, had let his hair grow because he hated having it cut. In the triumph of his shaky wellness she took him out into the yard and sat him in a kitchen chair in a light breeze that carried his curls away while he cried. He could tell this story and grow bored while telling it, smiling down at you with your head on the pillow, or wind a finger in your hair and tell you his hair had been as curly as *that,* or he could go rapt before a baseball game on the Magnavox, or he could drive away in the tail-finned Chrysler, or he could be a voice on the telephone asking you to please go get Mom. One way or another it was often a question of loving him from afar.

In the unevenly graded erasure of that hard black rubber sole was all the walking he did on the sidewalks in the city, where we didn't go except, unusual Sundays, to the zoo. *Why is a giraffe's neck so long? Because its head is so far from the ground,* cotton candy like sugar fiberglass drenching the tongue in hypersweetness, my brother and sister in strollers, sucking their thumbs relentlessly in every picture, though my mother trotted back and forth, plucking thumbs from mouths with audible *pops!,* trying to train a baby hand around a blue wooden bead or an enormous plastic key, browbeating and cajoling even as she focused, then sighing her sigh—"I give up"—because the two spit-glistening thumbs could not bear isolation and had slid back into their candy-flavored caves simultaneously while four eyes gazed at my mother without hostility but without any special regard, either. This was my chance to be the good child, to smile without blinking, and I ate it up, cotton candy for the zoo-stunned soul. My father said, "What's wrong with their sucking their thumbs?" "Oh, Eddie," my mother chided, which meant she was to suffer, at some bitter

future moment, for the truth of this moment, which he wasn't
helping her obscure. In slide after slide, on the ungainly screen
that traveled with us, in Kodachrome bright as hallucination
against the dimmed wallpaper in my grandparents' pulled-
shade living rooms, my brother and sister would gaze and gaze
unsmiling at those who most needed them to smile.

Now they were asleep. They had been asleep an hour. Over
each crib hung an untouched mobile, a pointless collection of
amazingly lifelike small birds. The mobiles were part of the
always-there world, and didn't fascinate. Dust motes in
Brownian motion fascinated, or a moth in its scalded dance
around the *I do love you* of the night-light, or any sound from
downstairs. Getting my brother and sister to relent and lie
down was a labor that brought out the worst in my mother.
She would go as far as wanting to wreak havoc with them,
growing scathing and sarcastic, as if they were powerfully
indifferent adults. Once down, they slept the night through
in a kind of soft, conscious-only-of-each-other (somehow)
sleep. They were as close as babies can be born without being
twins. Their small room deep at night had a charm that can
only come of children hotly embarked on sleep, so that my
mother, entering for a last check, could cry "Oh!" as if she were
stumbling through the woods and had seen human infants.

"*I* have to wash it," my mother said. "*I* have to get the
stains out before you wear that shirt again."

"Do you want this ring or not, Grace?"

His blindingly vivid—to me—resentment was his wanting to get down to work. How I feared what she was doing,
in stopping him.

"The stains!"

"Well?"

"Well, I don't want stains!"

His face, foreshortened downward, shaded jaw and pale,
black-lashed eyes, was angled to take us both in, my mother

and me. It didn't matter that I was maddened on his behalf; in his perception, we were mother and daughter. I couldn't have said what he was about to do, but he sat up, out of the box of shadow and enigmatic pipes, and with the clumsiness of private habit executed in public ran his fingers down the buttons. His undershirt's cotton was as translucent as an old handkerchief's. Under it showed his tiny, far-apart, embarrassing nipples, the single fold in his belly, and even the deep, unthinkable pit of his navel, squeezed shut horizontally. His shoulders were the same rashy, bridling red that appeared, more faintly, along his jaw after shaving. He had been on the brink of real fury, and pulling up short had left him shockingly graceful. He tossed the shirt underhand and she caught it and made vague gestures of folding. "Undershirt, too?" She nodded. He stripped, balled it up, and threw it to her. "Now do you want your damn ring?"

"How can you call it my damn ring?"

"Who lost it, Grace?"

"On purpose? On purpose, are you saying?"

"You tell me," he said, the upper, naked half of his body gone again, the lower half expressive of a workman's, mechanic's or plumber's, rich indifference to women, his legs crossed at the ankles.

"I made a mistake."

"A mistake," he said, his voice vaulted, his emotion backed up, boxed in, shaded, rare.

"I make mistakes!"

His fingers chased apprehensively around an octagonally faceted nut whose rusted-fast stubbornness I could feel from where I sat. He often said "It didn't take long for things to go wrong, did it?" and meant *with this house*. He wondered at what a fool he'd been, and also took pleasure in it, and I don't think he seriously regretted the move. Little things going wrong appeased his Depression-childhood conviction that he deserved disaster. Sure that something was wrong, he liked knowing *what* was. We'd lived here only two years but the electricity was often *on the blink,* and heating the place in winter *cost a fortune.* The little drafts that knew their way around the house smelled as frank and antidomestic as winter fields.

"You make mistakes!"

A change, an escalation—a defensive intensification, at least of tone, insanely timed to vex him, and I wondered what had happened: whether, hands submerged to the wrists, she could feel the brisk ride of the ring down her finger, and couldn't stop it; or whether she couldn't feel it, and had stared at her flushed, dripping, naked hands in shock.

He wasn't answering. The plywood floor of the cupboard still bore the lumberyard's inked stamps. We lived in a tract whose houses were uniformly pastel and cheap. I could recall writing my name in the grit, gratifyingly inexplicable, of our city apartment's windowsills, and that my father had been home more often, and home earlier, then, and that he had shushed me in bed, his finger to my lips, so that he and I could listen to the woman above us *traipsing*—his word—from room to room in her mysterious overhead replica of our floor plan. "High heels at all hours," my father whispered to me. He was pleased by her tirelessness.

Part of the point of this, the house we still called "the new house," was its distance from its identical neighbors. This distance had been calculated to suggest friendly independence, and was maintained in fresh-cut grass. Inside, the new house was strategically clean, as if vulnerable to inspection anytime. That was what was feared—you'd get a moment's notice before having to justify your life. Nobody visited—a law could have been passed in that suburb that nobody would visit back and forth except children—so the moment's notice was mythic, though no less exigent for that. A hopeless readiness prevailed in my friends' houses, too. Their living-room *suites* were also arranged to encourage conversation. All our mothers had read in magazines how to nurture conversation by the smart place-ment of furniture. They grew sullen with the repetition and simplicity needed by small children, and in their attitude toward conversation with other adults they were like saints who wanted wild animals to come and eat from their hands. They were going to remain pure and patient and immobile.

One or two houses still had the sweetness of freshly carpen-tered, unlived-in spaces, which I could remember ours having, and when I entered those houses I felt sick, as if I'd got lost. The subdivision's last empty lots, squared off with string, were of the same carbon blackness as the farmland that began after the final cul-de-sac. When we crossed these fields swinging our lunch boxes, crows battered into flight and wheeled around, anxious to get back to whatever they'd been picking at. All of us knew where there was a dead rabbit lodged under an aban-doned tractor tire, and we periodically visited its rotting until one morning a stray dog who'd been tagging after us seized the rabbit by its neck and dragged it out. The dog loped away with it and we didn't encounter him again, or we would have thrown clods for his having done that, wrestled the rabbit from its hiding place with such excitement. The farmer who owned this land hated our subdivision, and therefore us, so we ran when he was spotted in the distance. Or we stood together in the stark middle of a field with all our eyes closed until one of us pretended to hear him approaching and cried out and we scattered. He was a delight to us, as any feared adult who can be completely avoided is a delight and a boon to children. He plowed right up to the already-poured curbs, to the opulent black bays of virgin asphalt. He left hardly a milkweed to keep the pristine fire hydrants company. At dusk the new streetlights shone with dogged surrealism on rows and rows of stubble.

My father had pushed the under-the-sink clutter to the side he wasn't occupying. A can of Bon Ami had a chick on its label to prove how mild it was, and leaked a fragrance of acid cleanliness. The toothbrushes were ratty from polishing faucets, and I didn't like thinking they'd been ours. The sponges were rigidly dry, soiled with our family's trusting usual dirtiness. "You make mistakes!" she cried. There was the tarnished silver fork with crooked tines she used for poking around her houseplants, explaining that if the dirt got too tamped down the roots couldn't breathe. It was a fork she was fond of, which had been her great-grandmother's, a talismanically important fork from another country, devoted to this modest, satisfying task. The fork had not yet been lost. In spite of what she accused my father of, his recklessness in having been about to stain a shirt, and in spite of appearances in general, it was she who habitually misplaced possessions or ruined them. With my mother, care was a prized virtue haphazardly practiced.

She was forgetful, as women are whose ambitions, flawlessly carried out, still add up to nothing. When she made me a dress for a school play, I discovered only deep into the last act, when I was irrevocably committed to smiling muteness, that she had not hemmed the satin but only tacked it into place. She couldn't have guessed I would kneel right on the piercing line. I remained motionless, my knees seeming to saw down through an impossible fusion of satin and myriad-pointed pain, my heart beating beneath my Kleenex breasts, the hero and heroine waltzing the waltz that followed their kiss, dragging the spotlight after them. At that kiss, the dazzled mothers and fathers had laughed. They loved it so, that a girl child and a boy child would kiss. Flashbulbs went off, erratic, searing light from the dark expanse of parents, kind atomic bombs. It was so unmeant, that kiss, so unfelt by those kissing, that it belonged to the parents, it was their augury of perfect sexual felicity, which depended on determined searching, on the princely right to knock on any door, on woman after woman hating her own foot because it wouldn't fit, on carrying a glass shoe for miles on a cushion. If that shoe had been meant for me, my mother would have hemmed satin—oh, with joy, stitched the rustling sliding stuff as green light danced from it, with delight, the needle diving in and out, with pleasure because her daughter was about to illumine for an audience, as only a daughter can, the mother's perdurable beauty. Kneeling on those heartless points I understood her detachment. She would invest hope when I gave her some reason, but for now she was alienated. She was my sister's mother and my brother's mother—she could bend to them with the tenderness of a queen lighting candles, or scream at them like a flung-up crow, but at either extreme she was their mother. She wanted something from them, and all concerned knew it. She wasn't sure what to want of me at the age I was, ten. She would have liked someone to advise her, *Want this, be disappointed about that, hope for this change,* but there was no one with an overview. One night I heard her tell my father, "It's like loving *another person,*" by which she meant loving me was no longer like loving a baby. Belovedness showed in their blond indifference and in their quickness to console themselves and ultimately in my brother's and sister's distance from my mother. As long as she loved them wildly, they could take her or leave her. I had crazily little distance. When the spotlight careened across me, it showed a jealous sister.

Well: there was a forgotten dishrag, too, far back in the corner of the cupboard, a dishrag like a bird's nest left to wrack and ruin, withered mesh the gray of old grass, and there was also a marble, and a lost comb of my father's. "You make mistakes!"

Their somehow-decided-on rule was, third times got answers.

"Whose ring went down the damn drain?"

"Why do you care where that ring goes?"

"Hey, I'm through. I'm quitting. I wash my hands." He was coming out, his head ducked so it wouldn't strike the cupboard's overhang, his upward stare accusatory but not absolutely so—in fact touched with an apprehension I couldn't place, though he said, "If you want that ring back, you'd better call somebody. Do it quick before you forget and run more water through. I don't need this."

"This? This?"

He gestured—her, me, the kitchen, the entire house, none of it needed, none of it really needed, all of it costing too much. Stupidly, he yawned.

"Don't need it? No, you use it. *Use* it, that's your relation to this house. You come home like to a hotel! What do you know about what happens here all day? You might as well not come home at all!"

"O.K., you want me not to come back? You already got rid of your ring!"

"Good!"

"If I don't go after it now, you can kiss it good-bye!"

"Good!"

They gazed at each other, and I, gazing from the floor, nearer to my father than to her, aligned as I preferred to be but torn, feeling some shy breeze of remorse that wanted to blow me back toward her, toward the losing and therefore desperately loved side, couldn't tell when their mutual gaze changed, grew complex, complicitous, friendly. This was their saving grace: they could forgive so fast I couldn't tell exactly when it happened, much less why. Ordinariness flooded in around us, all three. They released each other from the spell of the fight. They might as well have taken several conciliatory steps back from each other, but they didn't. They couldn't, of course. He was still under the sink and she was backed up against the counter.

" 'Good!' " Dangerously, daringly, he quoted her to her-

self. He often told me, *Don't push your luck,* but his own luck
was elastic and serviceable after great abuse, at least his luck
with her.

"Eddie, you know I want my ring."

"No, I thought you could live without a ring."

"No, I can't. Of course I can't. Get it back for me."

I understood then how sweet a thing it was to want the
ring back—so sweet, it was like it was my ring.

"Get it back for you?"

"Get it back for me?"

And my mother, having had to ask this, looked seriously
at me, because only she and I could rightfully love my father
this recklessly. He had to remain remote, even indifferent. He
had to *not understand,* though I couldn't have said why, the
sensuous conviction she and I shared, which was that we
couldn't live without him, that we couldn't get through a day
without trusting him surpassingly in one matter or another.
His grunts encouraged the wrench, but its clasp wasn't exact.
He tried to get it to bite, but it slipped with a *ching,* and
chinged again, and he said "Damn" softly, and my mother and
I suffered, because that "Damn" was both grave and self-
pitying, which was how he sounded when he failed.

"Try another wrench," my mother said, and we experienced a wave of dislike—of us!—from my father, who pon-
dered the glittery recalcitrant U before tapping it, a hotheaded,
ringing blow with the wrench. "Son of a bitch. I know you're
in there."

She didn't like her ring being called "son of a bitch." "Try
another wrench, honey, O.K.?"

"Do you want me to get another wrench, Dad?"

His toolbox, lid ajar with a treasure chest's aplomb, waited
in a corner.

My mother told me, "Find another wrench."

He enlightened us. "I don't need another wrench. Don't

you think I know which wrench? It's just skiddy, and the nut's locked down real good. It must be the tightest thing in this house. This is the right wrench."

My mother squatted, she and I his watchers, his backers, his believers. He scrambled, shifting his weight for greater leverage, and the nut winced and whined and scraped through a rusty revolution, and he put it through another complete turn with a drone almost of shearing metal, and then he held the deep U, releasing its subterranean scent, in his hands. "Crawl out," my mother invited. "I'll get you something to dump it on." She spread shifty newsprint across gold-flecked linoleum. The front page, ironed flat with her palm, was Jackie Kennedy, and my mother paused. Jackie Kennedy had lost a baby. My mother swept this page aside. Voting for the Kennedys had left my parents solicitous toward them forever, and my mother had got her hair cut like Mrs. Kennedy. My mother's hair was rakish, bouffant, implausibly immobilized by a spray whose sting could bring tears to your eyes.

My father knocked packed gray dreck from the pipe. Two jolts with the heel of his hand tipped out a pyramid of filthy frayed confetti whose smell was calamitous.

My mother reached past my father, into the cupboard, for her fork, and diced through the mound. The reek forced her face away. She jabbed blindly for a minute.

"Oh, come on," my father told her. "You have to get in and dig." My sense that she had been weak and mincing vanished: she was upset now by the certainty that her ring *was* in that mess. It would almost have been better for it to have been gone. My father's hand, buried to the wrist, sifted, and his expression was simple, intent. So that was the trick. The ring had to be desired beyond nicety, beyond cringing. *He* had to find it. If she had discovered it while evincing loathing of the mess, the ring would have remained tainted. My father chose his moment. He was all for drama, now that he knew it would work out well. I think he actually found the ring a second, or several seconds, before he drew it out and displayed it, a circlet of air rimmed by smeared, glimmering, wet gold. My mother cried out, sank back onto her heels, and took it from him. For a moment I thought she might slide it onto her finger, rejoicing, but she carried it to the sink, started to turn on the tap, caught herself, and swabbed the ring clean with a dish towel. He wanted florid thanks, and she had—I read her back—forgotten he was waiting. She might have been close to crying. From behind she seemed to be having a long, private, decisive moment. Her decisive moments were often good: what got decided was that she would love us better, that she wouldn't lose her temper again, that she would throw a splendid birthday party for one of us and do the whole house up in banners and the smell of yellow cake.

He said, "From now on you remember to take it off, honey, O.K.?"

She worked it back onto her finger, I could see that. "I do remember."

"You didn't remember tonight, honey, did you?"

"I forgot once. Once!"

"How many *onces* do you think you get, honey?"

My mother dealt with him like this: flashing glances, distinctly separate, over her shoulder. Between those glances her gaze went back to the window, to an outside darkness so velvet and free of lights it was unusual, though our backyard ran down to the northernmost field of the hated farmer, and this window framed a view she liked because it was, so far, houseless, unsuburban, still farm. In her communion with the night outside lay the chance she could let this go, a chance as bright as her anger, competing against it without undermining it, in fact perversely enlivening it, as if she were still angrier because of the possibility that she could cease to be angry with him at all. She was sick with herself for not knowing how to *be* with him, furious or not angry in the least, but then, brilliant with decisiveness, she bolted through the back door.

Our kitchen floated in storm-door glass, a bright room suspended with scarcely a tremor against pitch-darkness before the door slammed behind her. My father clambered to his feet and with a hand between my shoulders urged me to the door so that we could look out. She ran past the laundry on the line, and I could feel my father get angry because she had left all his innocent shirts hanging, their arms helplessly flung wide in the darkness, pinned and wavering in repeated silent pleading. She dodged past without pitying his shirts. Where our lawn met the field, a boundary marked by forgotten strands of barbed wire my mother feared—they were rusty, I went barefoot—she stopped. This gesture I could interpret from behind, even from a distance, with no trouble. Pointed elbow, bent head, dexterous twist of the wrist. I knew before the ring flew across the field that it was gone.

My father kicked the door open so hard the storm glass almost went to shards—it hesitated, but didn't shatter. I caught the aluminum frame and levered it slowly back into place, a shut door behind the three of us. I felt suddenly much more *outside*. I followed my father. He was taking giant steps, but before each step he stopped dead to contemplate my mother at the lawn's end. Darkness redolent of mown grass enfolded us. He called, "What did you do?"

She blazed back at him. "I only did what you've been wanting to do!" She crossed her arms and held herself steady against remorse. She didn't know whether the greater guilt was to flare from within or without, but either way she was braced. She poured a little oil on the fire: "I'm not like you! I can't live in suspense! Go! Leave! Leave tonight if you want to!"

He took another step and cried, "I can't leave! I can't leave! I can't leave you!"

He had breached her composure. He had found the only words that could have made her unsure. Fear, foolishness, adoration—those were in the tension of her embrace of herself.

"No one can make me leave you!"

"You're not leaving?"

"I can't leave you!"

I recognized in my mother's stance, as children do, an image I was going to live with—began living with at once, really. Crossing that field to school, I was going to toe promising clods apart, sure one of them would break open on the ring, then sure the ring would shine in a fresh boot print, then convinced it would emerge in a gleam from the last dirty rag of snow. I began searching for it that night, after I was supposed to be in bed. I dropped my nightgown where our grass ended and stepped cautiously over the barbed wire into cold earth. The moon was so big the clods threw giant shadows, and the furrows were black streamers that sucked away toward a vanishing point. Little windows were the farmer's house, far enough away not to threaten. I don't know why I wasn't afraid of being seen or why I believed I had to be naked. I walked down a ridge spiked with corn stubble, between furrows as black as if oil had been poured down them, and let intuition dictate the place I should fall onto my hands and knees. I tried to discriminate between sharp and crumbling touches, to recognize *twig, leaf, pebble, stick,* but to my exaggerated awareness the field offered a hundred wedding rings. A moonlit dime, a bottle cap, occurred to me as round, real, inevitable, *it. There! Over there! No, there!* until I panted raggedly. A metal eyelet of the kind bootlaces thread through, the carapace of a dead beetle, a fragment of quartz. The field kept gleaming. I was farther and farther from our house. I couldn't believe the ring had flown this far. I cried from confusion, and when I was through crying I was cold.

Back in the house my scared conviction was *Something's*

wrong. I followed the sounds upward until I understood. They were making love. I crouched on the stairs, cold and scratched and dirty in my grass-fragrant nightgown, listening as if theirs were the voices of angels, as if they had come from elsewhere, and I didn't know them. I think I hated them then because they could save us, or not save us: because it was in their hands.

Kid Gentle

When she needed to say some-
thing just to hear the sound of her own voice, she said "Sam,"
struck to find his name on the tip of her tongue: she would
have reasoned she was so angry that his name would have
needed some summoning up, but no.

The stream rilling past Jenny's boots ran, with erosion,
the reflectionless soft café au lait of adobe. She waded with
what she told herself was caution, fearing submerged barbed
wire. Rain had sleeked her T-shirt to her skin, and each breath

was a brief-lived heartache, so cold was the air, so charged with ozone. The arroyo's far wall was washing out in a danger-ously deep arch, a red-clay cave marbled with exposed juniper roots and resonant with lapping water. Crouching, she counted twenty or more cigarette butts in a wobbling raft. The Delgado kids played in there, however often she asked them not to. Purely from self-consciousness Jenny was charming with chil-dren, absurd, conspiratorial; in consequence the dark-eyed tru-ant Delgados failed to take her seriously. Jenny dragged sandbags back into alignment in the low wall meant to stave off further erosion. The adobe slip that smoothed the burlap weave greased her freezing hands. The wall was useless. Sam needed to assess the damage and come up with their next move. *Sam* needed to warn the Delgados about keeping their three boys out of the arroyo, which flooded fast, often more than knee-deep, after rains like this evening's. The last time she talked to them, the two older boys stood pitching stones at a fence post while the smallest, who liked Jenny, stared ashamed at the toes of his sneakers. She was afraid for them: it had made her voice hard, frankly forceful, and of course they'd hated that—and still hadn't, the cigarette butts proved, listened.

Jenny sat heavily on a sandbag that soaked through the seat of her jeans. Her neck was bitten and, though she slapped, bitten again, mosquitoes working air that seemed too cold for them. From here a corner of the house was visible, though it was fading fast. The bedroom window, whose blue shutters were the secret reason she'd agreed with Sam to buy the house, wasn't lit. A trick she could have learned in ten days alone: leave a light on when you go out near dark. A scrap of paper blew shyly past her shoulder, winced and was alive, a bat after mosquitoes. Echoing back and forth between the arroyo's walls, more bats. Between clouds the moon emerged, the dazzling white of fireworks, to cast her shadow down running water.

Sam has been sleeping, with his army-surplus bag and a

borrowed futon, on the cement slab that will be the floor of a greenhouse, the roof already raised in bright blond two-by-fours. A cat crouches on Sam's chest at dawn, tucking its paws under and purring. The first time the cat's weight landed on his chest, Sam believed he was dying. "Dying?" "I wake up thinking *heart attack,* and it takes me a minute: *cat.* No, it's a cat. My heart's going *wham wham wham,* and gradually I figure out this means it's still working." He'd told this to Jenny long-distance last night, expecting her laugh, counting on her laugh, and what did Jenny say? "Are you coming home?"

"Ever?" he answered, and she noted the hushed exhalation that meant he was smoking a cigarette she would have bitched at him about if she'd been surer of his mood. He was calling from half an hour's distance, from the Santa Fe place of the couple whose greenhouse he was building. The greenhouse was ambitious, passive solar, and he'd told Jenny it could easily need another month. *Another month.* "How are you?" he asked. A Sam tactic: try acting as if nothing's wrong, and see if she'll take him up on it. This disingenuousness got them out of various scrapes, at least those neither of them wanted, or wanted badly enough, to be in.

"I hate the nights."

"You'll be fine."

" 'You'll be fine' is how you blow away whatever serious thing I've just said." She blew across the receiver, vehement illustration, and was surprised by a faint zinging reverberation, like a tuning fork's.

"Jenny, all I mean is I know you. You will be fine."

Fine alone? Or fine with you? is what she didn't ask next; *Maybe we need this time apart* is what she didn't provoke him into saying.

Jenny waded back down the arroyo and climbed the skiddy path between drifts of Christmas-tree scent that were wet junipers in the dark. Cascades from the gutters—*canales,* she amended—foamed down the footers for the porch—*portal,* in Spanish—she and Sam had imagined last winter, trading a napkin back and forth across a table homesteaded by their clutter of spoons and saucers, Jenny's gloves, Sam's watch cap, its navy wool glittering with the clear pinheads snowflakes shrank to in the close café warmth. A hundred futures for their house have appeared on napkins, torn envelopes, the backs of checks for two cups of coffee. However fitful, this was their deepest conversation, these sketches one or the other of them pushed away from the wet ring left by a lifted cup. They argued more or less softly. When she was pregnant, Jenny began drawing a child into the sketches. The child had an agile compact body and heavy, fair, straight, stick-straight bowl-cut hair that couldn't completely hide its too-large ears, but it didn't confront the viewer (her, Sam) directly enough to be definitively boy or girl. Before long it dawned on Jenny that she was repeatedly drawing the same child.

Something else occurred to Sam. "You draw a kid, never a baby."

"So?"

"So you skip the worst helplessness. The first year—entire, total dependency."

"You think I'm frightened." She was more interested than accusing, though she was a little accusing.

"I think you're smart to be frightened."

Just inside the front door, Jenny dropped her clothes in a muddied knot. Her jeans had grown skinny and cold and had to be weaseled out of. She stood pale, even in the dark, hugging herself. Ah: there was still, despite the storm, electricity. The bathroom went bright at a touch. She bathed in water so hot it was primally consoling, a cirrus of steam lolling from its surface, like a hot spring, with a hot spring's weary mineral taint, which was really the corroded-iron stink of the old pipes exposed in the wall she was meditating on. Nearly every project Sam undertook was initiated by a hole in the wall. Jenny towel-dried her hair into strings and hid her mirrored nakedness in clothes from the floor, leggings, undershirt, sweatshirt, socks, Sam's bathrobe. She remembered contemplating her ignorance after the little stick turned decisive blue. In the mirror, her tongue had gone to the corners of her mouth, she had tilted her chin this way and that. Her eyelids did seem subtly fattened, the definition of her hipbones blurred. The aureoles of her nipples had pinked and swollen. In their stems openings had appeared, tiny as tear ducts, in a ragged ring. *I can't believe it:* the vertigo of not having known some grand body change was taking place, the sense of being dragged forward in time, *not ready,* victim of a careening loneliness.

From that loneliness she cast forward. Eventually her certainty that she was going to die would be this sharp. Her soul would feel this tricked, this undercut. *But this is me! Me! You have to listen to me!* Her body had recognized its chance and closed around it like some gentle fist. *Tick tock,* Jenny thought, without happiness, and then, far too fast for any transition, with happiness. She knew herself, irresolute and thirty-six and full of trouble. If she wanted this, if she ever wanted this, now was the time.

When Sam said, "Do you want it?" she countered, "Do you?"

"Jenny, *Do you?* is the question."

(What did that mean?) (How much would he help?) "Not the only question."

"The first question."

It was clear from their voices, from the possessiveness of her arms around him, from the persuasive tenderness with which he ran a hand down her back to her bottom and up again, her forehead to his chest to hide what she thought, then her chin tipped up because she couldn't stand not knowing what he thought—but it was already clear, clear what they wanted, what they had learned, that minute, to want.

I, I, I went the fairy tale. You'd been listening ever since you could remember to *Now I'm going to* or *I changed my mind about* or *All I really need is,* absorbed in each twist and turn of the narrative. *I love*—you didn't know how to begin to perceive *I love* for what it was. Distrusting *I* constructions was tantamount to distrusting consciousness. Impossible not to believe that the universe—sun and moon and stars—swung around *I love.* "I do want it," in an amazed voice, was meant as an answer, was meant to decide the future. Miscarriage had taught Jenny: *I* could be so small, could be the magnet for a vast helplessness. *This can't happen to me* never stopped anyone's bleeding. She felt a fool, a freak, not to have known that. She was no longer a fool, a freak, a child.

The kitchen was an almost safe place, *almost* because she was acutely aware of being alone for the night. She set out a cup and saucer. As a child she'd made a game of passively letting the tears streak where they wanted, slicking her nostril wings, even creeping in, dampening breath, or beading on her upper lip and insinuating themselves into the corners of her mouth until they were a taste, searing fresh salt. Crying then finished in clear-eyed calm, even elation. Crying now is ugly, exacting, bitter through and through, monotonous from the beginning, ending in exhaustion. Sam said *Unreasonable,* he said *Come on,* he said *This can't be good for you, honey.* He said *honey* and something far, far down inside her went sweet. Whatever else she felt, something went sweet, as if a single leaf in an aspen tree flipped over and caught the light. That's how she keeps herself from crying now. He's not here to say *honey.* He can't seem to say it on the phone. It could be he needed her face to say *honey.*

The kettle shrilled. The tea bag bled itself an amber nimbus. Jenny drank, tucking dry cotton feet onto a chair rung, newspaper all over the table.

WEDDING DRESS, never been used, size 8 petite. $400. Plus veil. Josie.

Nobody tolerated, in a wedding, any whiff of previous failure, did they? Or could some couple believe their love impervious to the bad luck of a never-got-used beautiful dress? The wind was back, shivering the reflection of the kitchen in the big window, lofting the page of newsprint a hairbreadth from the table. Sam has said that window needs caulking.

> FOR SALE, small six-year-old Paint Mare, Pretty, goes English or Western. Asking $500 or best offer. Call Jim evenings.

Jenny had learned English, but Western was practical in Rio Arriba County's gopher-dug fields, washboarded dirt roads, and eroding badland bluffs. A painter, she liked "paint" used of a horse—liked, too, the cheerfulness of errant capitalization, and the confusion over whether the mare's name was "Pretty" or Jim just thought she was. Evening. This was evening. Getting late. Sam's calls, from the greenhouse couple's place, have been late, evasive, as coded and inconsequential as a boyfriend's. Maybe he became *husband* too young, so that *boyfriend* floated out there, a state whose possibilities hadn't been exhausted. The ring on Jenny's finger was eased on when she was twenty and he was twenty-two. She will have to learn *girlfriend* all over, the light provocativeness, the essential friendliness. This idea makes her feel tired and sad and heavy-handed.

She reread the ad's last line, finding it simple to lose interest. Sam had said, "*Borrow* a horse, then," sounding like himself again in his impatience with her. She skipped past cords of piñon, ten-speeds, chain saws, tipis, and automatic baby swings to:

> FOR SALE, good mountain and pleasure horse, 5 years old, QH type, good disposition and solid dark feet. For an intermediate rider, $700. Leave message for Rick.

Jenny liked this horse for standing so foursquare on his solid
dark feet. What she suffered was attraction: here was such
calm. His lip cringed up like a chimpanzee's, elastic, whis-
kered; his teeth closed on her weed bouquet. He jerked at
the leaves with restrained ducks of his heavy head, broad for
braininess between the ears—Rocky, his name was. A ten-
year-old in a baseball cap had guided Jenny to this field, and
was waiting, still straddling his dirt bike, a presence she
wished she could ignore, because it was a kind of lie, or at
least an act, for her to be here. In a fit of blackly descending
detachment, she knew she couldn't buy the horse. She lacked
the energy to return to the trailer and carry on the nice, vague,
glancing negotiation with the boy's father—Rick—that would
have shaved some amount from the seven hundred asked-for
dollars. Actually, the boy's father hadn't been alone in the
trailer, but with another man, like enough to be his brother
or cousin, and they'd been making breakfast, an entire refrigerator's profusion emptied onto the kitchen table, jars of jala-
peños, mayonnaise, and salsa, an onion minced right onto
Formica, a carton to which the broken eggshells had been
returned, a cigarette left burning in a jar lid gleaming the
broken-glass purple of grape jelly. "Can you cook?" Rick had
gestured helplessly with a spatula. *This is a mess.* "You look
like you're doing fine," Jenny said. Rick studied her up and
down. She supposed she looked tense, standing there in her
T-shirt and jeans, hands shoved deep into her pockets, a boyish
pose, defensive; in fact, she couldn't have said what she was
doing there, or how she was going to get out of there, but
Rick unexpectedly helped. "If you can find my kid, he'll take
you out to that horse we're selling."

Now, "Aren't you going to ride him?" the boy demanded.
He yanked his bike around and pedaled hard to catch her. "I
just remembered something," she said foolishly. "What?" he
cried, "What?" incredulous as a conscience at what she was

doing. She worried he wasn't watching, the dirt road all ruts
and stones, but he jarred along gymnastically. She avoided the
trailer stranded on its cinder blocks, but starting her Volkswagen she had to recognize, through the windshield, the boy's
disappointment. He didn't wave. She had, obscurely, no right
to leave.

A dusk without rain, but growing steadily colder, kindling
by the wood stove but no fire lit, tea in its cup by Jenny's
elbow. The dark-footed gelding finally disappeared from the
want ads a week ago.

> SIX-YEAR-OLD chestnut Quarter Horse mare,
> nice mover, reliable. $500. Call evenings.

Not sinful, wanting a horse, but inexplicable, in Sam's view.
Or, Sam's code for the irrational, "Not something we need."
Their road winds down a hill, two dirt ruts with a central
mane of parched grass, and where it passes Delgado's and
Salazar's orchards it's so narrow Sam's truck is raked by twigs,
and he finds apples in with his tools. Sam's gunning of the
engine at the foot of the hill is the single familiar sound the
night withholds. She knows the phone won't ring. It rang last
night, and before they got very far, their mutual evasiveness
fell through—collapsed into tension so flagrant she asked,
"What do we do now?"

When he said nothing, Jenny caught herself rehearsing an
answer for him: *We try again, O.K.?*

In the space of a held breath, this little inward voice
instructed Jenny in her amazing answer to that answer: *Oh, I
want to, too.*

"What do we do now?" was still waiting, and it was what
he answered, obliquely. "You're so angry at me."

She was scared to find herself so alone, and turned on him with consummate scornful patience. "Because you act like this didn't happen, or like it happened only to me. I dream about it, did you know that? I dream about you not getting there."

"Jenny. This isn't the time. I can't go into it."

"Of course you can't."

She'd meant to hurt. Another wary, hidden-from-her exhalation. He smoked more when he was away, and kept the clothes in his duffel neater than in his drawers in their bedroom dresser, and bought lottery tickets. He told her he was tired, and when she said she knew that, he said, "Too tired to come home."

> SIX-YEAR-OLD Thoroughbred mare, race winner at Santa Fe Downs last spring. $400. Call Mack.

The cost of Josie's wedding gown plus veil, and "Thoroughbred" functions as a one-word seduction. *You're not thinking,* Jenny told herself. *Not using your head.* Sam's stress on *using.* Anyone could own a cliché through sheer idiosyncracy of inflection. Jenny's doctor had warned that they should not rush themselves, but give each other *time.* Boxed, wrapped, ribboned, to be exchanged like anniversary gifts, or did Dr. Chavez mean time was an element they were to share, like the oxygen you both breathed when you lived in the same house, like a bed? The cup rang in its saucer. She couldn't guess how destructive last night was. The injury's dimensions were shadowy because it had occurred in Sam.

The morning after they became lovers, Sam broke two fingers in touch football with his housemates, and because she'd been sitting on the sidelines, barely awake but on the verge of disenchantment anyway—he'd seemed the silliest, the least familiar, of seven boys—her morning-after doubt abandoned her. She had to drive him to the hospital: he was hers. The doctor told Jenny, "Here's what's going on with your boyfriend." Who was she—Girlfriend, after one night? Lover?—to be shown his X rays? Nobody had thought she should be uneasy, seeing inside, seeing irremediably deep, seeing slender bones. He said, "What's come over you?" when they made love that night. He said, "What is it?" so tenderly. What had come over her was fear. He was real to her, and she wasn't real to him yet.

He would say that the skittishness with which the mare observed this stranger, Jenny, was proof of the continual singing of the nerves that wrecks Thoroughbreds. The mare's owner, end of a blond braid showing under her riding helmet, coaxed the mare's nose into the bridle cat's-cradled between her hands, then let the reins drop to the mare's withers, which flinched, even that lightly struck.

"I should warn you," the woman, Lindsay, said. Mack didn't exist; Lindsay hadn't wanted any crazies on the phone. "It took me half an hour to catch her." She rested a palm judgingly on the mare's chest. "Feel."

The slickness was like a wet dog's, muscled, hot, holding a potent faraway heartbeat. Sweat stung a paper cut. Jenny sucked the finger and heard herself: "I haven't been on a horse in so long."

"Really? Is the bad girl who you want to start with?"

"Bad girl?"

"Cortez's Shining Daughter, her papers say. Shiny Little Bitch when I can't catch her. The bad girl."

"She's beautiful."

"That's the thing." Lindsay was bumped a step forward, butted from behind. "Horse for 'Can we please rock-and-roll?' "

Jenny recollected, then, that people who hung around horses liked making up dialogue for them. "Why are you selling her?" This wasn't rude, Jenny figured, not given this coyote-fenced paddock, the lap pool in the distance, the architecturally inscrutable house—adobe saltbox?—beyond that. She had parked her VW beside a baking black Mercedes, and felt fraudulent.

Lindsay said to the horse, "Me kiss you good-bye? Can that happen? Is it really a question?"

Jenny assumed the last question meant her. "If you want it to be," Jenny said. "I like her."

"You're still on the ground."

Jenny, given a leg up, hoped this mocking observer couldn't tell how unsure her seat was. Her hands transmitted an unfamiliar tension, at which the mare's ears flattened. *"Anh-anh-anh,"* Lindsay chided, handing up the black-velvet helmet, still warm from her head, a secure fit, Jenny's jaw daintily underlined by the strap. Jenny dug her heels in harder than she meant to, and the mare startled into a canter, ears clicking forward to frame a movie of the ground, sage and junipers reeling past foreshortened, dust acrid on Jenny's tongue, a sly panic rising. The mare perceived mistrust, which was incorporated into her canter as an imprecision, the not entirely innocent threat that she'd put a foot wrong. Jenny relaxed hands and knees, faking a confidence the mare bought. Her canter settled, the field was crossed, space flung itself out- and grandly outward, as if in reaction to them, space set off like rings radiating from a skipped stone, like fast, serial touches of stone across water, and Jenny, remembering it completely as she felt it again, had the sweetly fearless sensation of loving speed. The fence rose before them, the mare cornered neatly, and a magpie flared from a juniper. The mare jarred sideways, dodging the bird and then dodging from haywire momentum, and Jenny was seized by a long, weightlessly pure moment of grief. Her shoulder smashed first and she rolled, fearing hooves, hoofbeats concussing the ground she was sliding across, her forearm in front of her face, grinding on knees and elbows across sun-warmed gritty dust that threw at her a cholla, a prickly pear, before stony gravity fixated on her, before the silently dilating, slowly steadying earth let her lie there. A line of ants wound past her nose in huge close-up, bearing a butterfly wing, a backlit yellow shard, scarcely trembling. The ants that followed carried the butterfly's antennaed head. Jenny sat up, holding her wrist, trying her fingers. In her bathroom, Lindsay doled out Tylenol before concentrating on the arm Jenny extended.

"I'm a coward," Jenny said.

The thorns were as wickedly elusive as fish bones, translucent but, unlike fish bones, rigid, bristling. Lindsay said tensely, miserably, "Ow," each time she nicked one free. "What's this?" Tweezer tips indicated linked hives.

"Red ants."

"For somebody who didn't get hurt, you got hurt."

"Do you think it needs a doctor?" Jenny asked, a question met somewhat blankly by Lindsay's wide, pale, appraisingly practical face.

"I can do this."

"O.K."

"If you trust me to."

Like all people who ask you to trust them, she was a little offended. "O.K."

"Bear with me. *Ow*. Can you hold any stiller?"

Relief washed through Jenny, seated on the john with nothing more to do. All around them, Mexican tiles sported small blue birds, naïvely painted, their wings spread wide. Jenny dashed off wings, curved breasts, swallowtails in rapid dozens; she lived in a sunstruck Mexican village and she made her living painting exactly the same bird again and again and she was never coming back. It was too nice knowing just what would happen next.

"Done. Now for your face." Lindsay lifted Jenny's chin,
Jenny shutting her eyes against the painful glare that was the
skylight. Lindsay washed Jenny's face so gently that Jenny felt
acutely childlike. She felt shaken by such a dose of tenderness,
as only an adult can be shaken.

In her kitchen, Lindsay poured scotch into tumblers.
"Cliché," she said.

"Cliché?"

"Doctor's wife drinks away the lonely afternoon. That was
your first ride in how long?"

"I don't really drink," Jenny said. "Years. I'm on her back
two minutes, maybe."

"You fell well, you know. Not everybody can, not even
good riders. Do you remember Jackie Kennedy calling Jack
in a rage because paparazzi caught her landing on her rear?
He says, 'Honey, if the First Lady falls on her ass, it's news.'
He was what none of them are now, funny."

"I loved him."

"God, I loved him."

"I cried."

"God, I cried."

"Then we find out about Marilyn Monroe."

"Then we find out about everyone. Well," Lindsay said,
"to news," and they chinked glasses.

"You're not telling me to go out there and get right back
on."

"Nope. I'm for getting back on when you want to."

Lindsay poured again, talking—the worst tricks Cortie
had played on her; other, truly vicious horses she'd known;
falls she'd seen. "It's a lot to ask." Lindsay brooded over scotch
barely paled by Perrier. "You're all right, and she's all right."
Jenny grew increasingly dreamy in Lindsay's gleaming, finished kitchen. No holes in the walls in this house. Maybe this
was what Sam got from being away. The details of other

people's lives were a distraction surprisingly intense, as if you'd secretly believed your own depression had starved everyone else of vitality. Here was Lindsay, saying, "A bite," scratching at a shoulder, then savaging it with French-manicured nails, here were the blond strands that wavered, buoyed by static electricity, from her loosening braid, and past her shoulder the dish towel hanging from the oven door, a shadow replicating each fold, further, infinitesimally scaled shadows cast by each pane in the waffled cloth, like the tranquil iteration of cells across a honeycomb, the compounding of facets in a butterfly's eye, cratering of rain in a stream, the transcendent perfectionism of the world, which Jenny had trusted, which had, in her body, miscarried.

"You have kids?"

"Two of my own—ours—plus one from Kenny's first marriage, who lives with us. You?"

"We want one," Jenny said. "I think we want one."

The ambiguity attracted Lindsay. She leaned forward over her own crossed arms. Jenny had found that her friendships with women often began this way, with an ambiguity threaded into small talk. If the ambiguity was taken up, then something would follow. The conversation would make a mutually acknowledged, though small, gain in seriousness. Between women, a neglected ambiguity was a rebuff. Between men, it was a courtesy. Therefore, when you see a man and a woman talking together—

Lindsay touched Jenny's wrist to ask, "Does it still hurt?"

—you laid the groundwork for disappointment—

"Hurt much, I mean?"

—incomprehension, recrimination—

Jenny interrupted her own slightly woozy line of thought. "No. Yes. Not really. You were so patient. I can't thank you." She remembered she was supposed to add *enough*. "Thank you enough."

"For a minute I was afraid we'd have to call my husband."

"He's a doctor?"

"The worst, an o.b., gone all the time, and when he's here he thinks I should be like a patient, and adore him. He has trouble with the little daily stuff, and I agree, a lot of what I feel is not adoration."

"What's his name, though?"

"Kenny. Chavez. Do you know him?" She set her tumbler down. "You do. You know him. He's your doctor."

"He's my doctor," Jenny said with a lilt.

"Well—what does he say, about your wanting a baby? He likes to tell women your age—you're thirty-five?—to get with the program. He can be crude."

"He said, Wait before trying again. He was *kind*. I had a miscarriage at five months."

"I'm sorry, I'm so—" Lindsay shook her head. "Such a—"

"It's all right. It is. It was seven—it was eight weeks ago."

Lindsay said, "But isn't two months what Kenny told you to wait before trying?"

Jenny wasn't disturbed that she'd forgotten; she was disturbed that, under a veneer of forgetfulness, she'd known so exactly. *I want to, too.* "You're right."

To the hospital: Jenny, wearing the sweatshirt and torn jeans she cleaned house in, had tugged her cowboy boots on over dirty bare feet to go out. In the Pojoaque 7-Eleven she bought Windex and the newspaper and a Hershey's bar she ate two bites of before clicking off Van Morrison so she could concentrate on the interval of disbelief that followed the first pain, and then—oh, fear took her over, and she let it, because she thought fear might know what to do. One downward-dragging menstrual rush followed another, and Jenny thought, *I can drive, it's fastest,* but she couldn't imagine walking to EMERGENCY, which was red letters through falling rain. She let the wipers sweep their half-moons and the engine idle and the headlights keep pouring into the rain until somebody knocked at her window—an orderly, still in his hospital greens, who'd been taking a cigarette break. He helped her. Dr. Chavez had been in the hospital, making rounds. Alone at last, Jenny found the hostile room nearly dark. Her miscarriage had absorbed the light, like a day's work. They had given her something (a lot of things). She curled up, bare feet and gown and sheets and pillowcases quite clean, curling into herself, into the plush cozening of the drugs. During the night a slit widened into a doorway in which her doctor, like a half-dreamed, half-seen father come home late, stood studying her. "You're awake. Good. I'll get Sam." Sam, illumination from the hallway allowing her to piece together, in quick, slanting takes, the angles and shadows of his face. She was sure she was incoherent, but he answered, "Jenny, you can't believe that."

"I didn't want him enough. Not enough."

"Sweetie, sweetheart, shit, this wasn't about wanting. This was just a bad thing that happened."

"I didn't love him. Not all the time."

"You loved him. Let's not do this so late at night. Let's really not. Go back to sleep. I'll hold you, all right? I'll hold you, but you need to *Shhhhhhhh. Shhhhhhhh.*"

Dr. Chavez had said the next morning, "We hope we don't get this situation. We like to determine a cause, because that's better all round, so I'm sorry. As far as I know there's nothing wrong with Jenny, and there was nothing wrong with the baby." He'd stopped, anticipating Sam's anger.

"We don't get to know why, and you can't rule out the same thing happening again."

"I'm afraid that's the shape of it. But chances are very—"

Dr. Chavez had gone on, Jenny no longer listening. A nurse, less circumspect, from urgent kindness, than the doctor in this morning's conference, had told Jenny the night before that the baby was a boy.

"I've got to go," Jenny said.

"Oh, I think you need coffee." Lindsay set the kettle on the burner. Jenny knew from magazine ads that the kettle was in a design museum somewhere. Even in her sweaty, horsey T-shirt, Lindsay was fresh, together, somehow visibly rich. Envy, Jenny told herself: that's ugly. Considering Lindsay's kindness, it seemed a new low point. Lindsay poured coffee into glass mugs transparent even to their handles. "Cream?"

"Yes. Thanks." Cream rolled through the ragged explosions of time-lapse roses. "Know why I'm selling her?"

"Selling her. Liar."

"Kenny expects to happen to me what happened to you, only more serious. He claims it distracts him. Some days, he says, that's all he thinks about, me lying in the field hurt, when his mind has to be on what he's doing."

"There's nobody very nearby if you did get hurt."

"I can tell him I tried to get rid of her. That might help calm him down. Listen, you don't have to be looking for a horse to come back."

"I'd like to." Jenny stood, waiting for her head to clear, and was led through a living room done in Saltillo tile and teak and taupe leather couches. The walls were Rothenberg, T. C. Cannon, a sullen Scholder, the front doors massive and carved, long ago stolen from somewhere. Lindsay said, "Will you call?"

"Or you can."

"You're in the book? Your last name's—?"

"Small."

Lindsay said, "You're a painter."

"Right." Jenny was confused. They'd talked about her being a painter, in the kitchen.

Lindsay dragged her back through the room, past a grand piano crowned by a vase of calla lilies. How to get your money's worth out of lilies: have them twice, once real, once reflected in the oil slick of a grand piano's lid, Jenny thought, before she was aimed at a wall where there hung a small drawing she had done two years ago—the bedroom window, the Taos blue of its shutters barely figuring in the composition, which was mostly soft umbers and burnt sienna. The window was open a few inches. You could see, though not far, into the dim interior, the wide planks of the floor, the corner of a bed, the cross-hatching that was a nine-patch quilt, and, scarcely there, merest suggestion, the intertwined legs of a couple. Lindsay said, "It's a tiny daydream, not a drawing. It happens in my head."

"My dealer didn't want it, really. Then, when she sold it, I couldn't ask to who. I missed it."

"Why I bought it—this sounds silly—was because I could cover it with my hand. Make it go away, make it come back, with my hand, and it kept being beautiful." Lindsay paused. "Do you want to borrow it? You said you missed it."

"No. I'm just glad to see it again."

At Lindsay's front door they said, "Well—"

"Well—"

They parted awkwardly, new friends.

Sam came home that night, tense and formal, ready to be patient with her, but it happened that both of them desired an evening without confrontation. It wasn't as strange as it should have been, by any rational scale, to lie aimlessly talking to him again in bed. It hadn't felt as strange as it should have to make love. Their attraction to each other had often enough seemed simple, precipitous luck. Jenny didn't want to question it. She said, "I sold a painting." The message had been on her machine.

"Which?"

"The pale-green apples on the windowsill with our hill in the background."

"But that's huge." Sam often thought of her work in terms of size—of money, really.

"To a couple from Fort Worth, Angie said, who have lots of brand-new bare walls."

"Walls needing paintings?"

"They like me, Angie says."

"People from Fort Worth like you. Rich people like you."

"Uh-huh. Oh, you have to talk to the Delgados. They don't like me. They like you."

"Well, I'm more easygoing."

She said, "Will you?"

"I already did. I passed Juan on the road. I said that arroyo keeps flooding. He said he'd get after his kids about it." He lifted her arm from the sheets, and would have run his thumb deftly down the line of rash if she hadn't jerked away. She said, "You have to fix those stairs."

The wooden stairs down the slope to her studio, she meant. He had often wondered if those stairs were all right. Prickly pear grew close against them, and it was a believable scenario. He said, "Jesus. Meanwhile, can you be careful?"

She didn't tell Sam she was looking for a horse, and he was gone in the morning before she was awake enough to be vulnerable to questions. She got kissed, and smelled coffee, and woke again an hour later alone. Leaning to pick his shirt up from the floor, Jenny felt generous and capricious and consumed by curiosity about what would happen next: in love. "We need to talk," she told his shirt. When she held it to her nose there was a carpenter's day—cut wood, sun, breezy sweatiness.

Jenny in her nightgown, 2:00 a.m., read of Chevy pickups, wicker love seats, roof shingles, CD players, sets of encyclopedias and outgrown skis; well drilling, bail bonding, marriage licensing, engine rebuilding; guitars, violins, banjos, and mandolins adrift in the Chagall-like night sky that was the true backdrop of want ads everywhere; vacant spaces for trailer homes with complete service hookups; Sikhs to guard warehouses; child care in my home, Christian atmosphere, Navaho rugs restored to their original beauty.

> GREEN broke quarterhorse colt, $550 unfinished, $650 finished. Also kid's pony, make offer.

> HORSES: one chestnut gelding, $750. One black filly, halter broke, $200, or deal on the pair. Call Larry after 5 or all day weekends.

What was Sam thinking? It's been two days since their night, and he hasn't called. When she gets in from the studio, PLAYBACK yields a dozen voices, none of them his. Though she was seated in a solid chair, though she could identify every sound the night offered, though she'd washed every dish in this kitchen a thousand times, this was the disorientation of crushed expectations. She cupped her tea's heat between her palms, drank, and found:

> PUREBRED, registered Arabian gelding, broke, kid gentle, $800 cheap.

" 'Kid gentle' means?" Jenny asked the man—early Saturday, and he had a shy, maybe hung-over unkemptness, unshaven. The black hair, combed straight back, still wet from the shower, was a little embarrassing, as if she were seeing him at the wrong time or in a too-intimate way, as only a girlfriend should. She caught herself thinking *girlfriend,* not *wife.* He was the kind of handsome Jenny qualified privately as *almost too.*

"What it sounds like." He hoisted his four-year-old, and the boy, in his loftiness, touched the horse's nose. His fingers got snorted on, and he giggled. He put his fingers into the horse's mouth, its upper lip fluttering accommodatingly upward, then reached for its ear and worked it like a lever. "Jase, you let go now," the man, Carlos, said. "I think you proved my point." To Jenny he said, "Want to ride him?"

"I'd like to."

"Can you keep my kid from getting stepped on a minute, and I get the saddle?"

"Sure."

Jenny sat cross-legged, sun very warm on her back. The little boy took a slice of sugar toast from the plank in the fence where he'd left it balanced. "Let me see," Jenny said, and shook an ant from it, and a brief rain of sugar. "You know that was a red ant, don't you?" she said. "Look. They got me." He considered her garish arm, fascinated, then turned his toast over and over before taking a bite. Jenny felt a rising happiness, the grass blowing around them, level fields running down to a wash brimming with spring cottonwoods, the mesa opposite the red of cayenne pepper, and the boy said, "He's my mom's horse."

"Oh? Your mom's?"

"She wants to live in Albkirky with no room for a horse. We don't know if we go with her or not."

"Hey, are you telling all our secrets?" The father ruffled the boy's hair, leaning slightly, balancing the saddle against his side. "Are you going to be just like I am with pretty women?"

Jenny laughed. The child, confused, serious, laughed. When she was in the saddle, Carlos measured the stirrup leather against Jenny's extended leg, and though she wished she didn't, she liked that. Carlos kept a hand on her knee, pointing. "You can go as far as you want down that dirt road, see if you understand each other. All that's our land, but the neighbors won't mind if you get a little past it. He can't get lost."

"What a good quality." She thought he should probably take his hand off her knee now, and he did.

"This is a good horse I'm selling you."

"What's his name?"

"We never named him. Had him how long?, and never did. It seems funny now, but he was just 'the horse.' It's not like we had twenty. I can make one up for you if you want."

"No, thanks."

The horse had a smart canter, chin down, ears pricked. His style was unassuming and mindful. She gave him a little more leg. His new speed, matched by a fractional gain in interest, was just as judicious. He'd be unlikely to put a foot down one of the gopher holes in the bluffs behind Jenny and Sam's house, or shy at barking dogs. Jenny was under no illusion that the gelding experienced anything like the improbable affection she felt for him—Why should he?—but he had sweet manners, willingness, quick wits.

"Can I have some time to watch him?" Jenny asked, when she got back, and Carlos grinned—though this time the grin was a shade conscious in its appeal—before saying, "Buy him. Then you get a lot of time to watch him," taking his son by the hand, and leaving her there. Jenny rested against the fence, following the horse's methodical grazing, the muscled slant of his shoulder, the way he put his nose into the grass and nudged once, twice, so that the small bees were driven out.

"Yes," she said at their back porch. She got high fives from father and son alike, and sat beside them on the steps to write out the check. Carlos leaned back on his elbows, his son between his wide-apart knees. "He comes with his tack," Carlos said, "and my feeding him until you come for him, I throw that in for free. He trailers real nice."

"I wonder," Jenny said.

This attracted a slantwise doubtfulness; Carlos thought she could have changed her mind. "Un-hunh?"

"Can I keep him here?"

"Here?" Impolite to ask, directly, *Why?* "It's a drive for you."

"Twenty minutes. I'll come a couple of times a week. I mean"—the pause was awkwardness—"not for long. Until I find a place closer to home for him."

Carlos said, "That's our field. Nobody's using it. You can if you want to."

"Really?" She didn't know how to sound properly grateful—enough, not too much, not stupidly but gracefully appreciative.

"Sure. Really. He's happy here. Getting a little fat, maybe, but you can work that off him. Want some coffee?"

She raked strands of her hair from the corners of her mouth, where the wind had blown them, as it was blowing Carlos's drying hair, as it was blowing around his son's. She wanted a cup of coffee, a kiss, a life she knew inside and out—wanted, with an absurd passion, this man, this child, this place. Who would she be if she let that show, if she went inside, if she had a cup of coffee?

"No," Jenny said, "I think I'd better go," and she and Carlos shook hands.

That night, Sam came home. He sat across from her, the table between them lit by a citronella candle. She supposed that if they ever came to an agreed-on break—separation, divorce—Sam would cook for that occasion, too, and they would discuss it like friends. For a lark, he'd dragged their rickety outside table into the middle of the imaginary *portal.* Beneath their bare feet, warm, turned earth. Stars were out.

"So you went ahead and did it." He didn't want to sound so angry. He was too far in the wrong to carry such anger off.

"It was my money."

"It's not only money." The half-coyote mongrel of their neighbors across the arroyo, the Quintanas, leapt the footer, sat and whined, and Sam tossed him the skin of his grilled chicken breast, gone in a snap, and then a heel of French bread the dog trotted off with.

"We'll have ten dogs here."

"Naw, he can keep a secret." Sam poured more wine. "I don't want you keeping the horse that far away."

"Oh, you don't want me."

"You'd be gone all the time. It would turn into something."

She said, "Your being gone, what did that turn into?"

"It turned into me right here. I'm home." He could do this, go from antagonistic to charming, skipping conciliatory altogether. She still expected the concessions she would have made, in his place—the strategies to disarm, to rationalize.

She said abruptly, "How sad were you, Sam?"

"You really want to talk about it?"

"That's just one question."

"If I wasn't as sad as you, I lose you?"

"If I don't know you anymore, do you have me?"

"All right. How sad was I." His voice was absolutely careful. "I thought, before this happened, that we would always be fine. I didn't know you could be in pain, and I wouldn't even know—that I'd only get to you hours later. I never believed in my mind we were exempt, but I'm trying to tell you, I was living as if we couldn't be touched."

"Other things have happened."

"Not like this. It was finding out I'm not the person who can protect you. I don't know if I thought about the baby as much as I thought about you. Maybe I can't take care of anything, I don't know. I don't know what we do, I don't know what comes next, and you—that's what you want to ask me, isn't it? 'What do we do now?' "

"Yes."

"Maybe we don't plan. Maybe we just see."

And did he mean a baby, or did he mean see what things were like between them? It was their usual accord, spoken only to a certain point, trusted—she feared—only to a certain point, but though they spent their days apart, they went to bed together, and before long she knew she was pregnant. She waited to take the test, she waited to tell him—waited, spending the long afternoons riding, or in the Quintanas' two-stall shed, long unused, where the gelding was kept, for now. Under the corrugated tin roof, the straw-fragrant heat formed a room of its own, stifling, luxurious. Dust fumed from the chestnut flank. The currycomb scoured in circles, the brush followed the grain of the hair. The hoof-pick flaked chips of gravel from the massive, upturned bowl of bone weighting her knee, her thigh, her entire side. She rested a palm against his neck—like satin flushed from within by a sunlamp. His neck quaked when flies landed, his head lifted and was shaken irritably, the large eye vulnerable, lashed in languid flies. She swept her hand across it, making the eye blink and flies shoo. She didn't know if anything was changing, if trust could accumulate, or—it seemed far more remote—affection, but she was sure kindness had to be gestural here, consistent, patiently repeated. One morning, later than usual, she shoved the gate open to find the Delgados' smallest boy under the horse, playing with *Star Wars* figures in a cave, in shade aglint with motes of straw, anchored at its four corners by immobile hooves. The horse flirted its ears nervously at Jenny, who said softly, "You're doing great. You're doing fine," and bent until the boy granted her his attention. His upward gaze had the uncomprehending felicity of a child getting away with some-

thing dangerous. She told him to come out slowly, and he
came in a sneakered half crouch, the crown of his head brushing
the horse's belly but not distracting the horse from his deliber-
ate delicate motionlessness.

Jenny caught the boy's wrist and knelt down. Facing her,
he got scared at last and clasped her neck, leaning into her as
she leaned her cheek against his hair, and they waited. What
could have happened withered and grew incredible and blew
away, leaving them alone, her arms around him and his arms
around her.

The Minute I Saw You

In the airport as he's leaving for California his dad catches him off guard with a kiss and a warning: "Don't date any girls named Squeaky." Lately Kevin has come up with a new way of dealing with his father's sense of humor—a laugh, then a step back and a black-leather-jacketed shrug. Ironic acquiescence to the distance between them—or so Kevin explains it privately, to himself. That's what his father wants, and why his jokes are always so absurd, so un-fieldable. If Kevin let him, his father would dead-end every conversation between them with some such surrealistic line. The aspect of this Kevin sometimes forgets is how much the dead-ending tends to hurt, how fast it reduces him to childish lostness at not understanding his father. Kevin doesn't need that, not when he's finally doing what his stepmother, Caro, refers to as "getting out of the house for a month, thank God." It's not that there's trouble between his stepmother and Kevin. There's not, or nothing specific, but she has the baby to deal with now, a furious, colicky, chapped-red girl for whom Kevin has a secret store of nicknames. Milk Leech. Live Afterbirth. Amoeba. It's like trying out ugly names for a band. He's risked aloud only "Brat," which made Caro smile in a distracted flash of her old, prebaby self. "She kind of is," Caro said. This morning when Kevin went in to tell her he was leaving, she was profoundly unconscious, strands of her hair glued by dried milk to the sleeping baby's lower lip, a connection Kevin broke gently, surprised when the baby's head jerked around and his finger was enveloped in a warm, small-scale, imploring vacuum, though those eyelids, sealed tight, expressed only sleep, deep sleep and ethereal unawareness. The lively little *suck-suck-suck,* undercutting that dreaming blandness, tricked Kevin into his first and only rush of helpless tenderness toward his sister. He withdrew his giant hand; the baby sighed and jammed a fist against her still-open mouth. Kevin leaned closer to Caro's ear: Chanel No. 19 and lanolin, to name two of her smells. "I miss you." The feeling of missing her while she slept caused him to say this, not to her but to her submerged, alert subconscious, the way movies used to be spliced with decisecond images of popcorn.

His father drove Kevin through the slowly brightening desert. Kevin and his father have had almost no time alone since the baby was born; throughout the two-hour drive Kevin had pretended sleep; just now, in his father's embrace, Kevin experienced his own body as solid, grown, as resistant to his father's touch as another man's should be.

"I won't meet any girls named Squeaky."

"That's the thing." His father's tone is of rueful parental one-upmanship. "You will."

Everyone milling past them, parting or greeting, knows how to do this much better than they do, and they can't stand here much longer, awkwardness compounding like this. Kevin shifts on sneakered feet and gives his backpack a hitch, as if to lift it. He and his father have never been able to carry off the minor public rituals.

"What I mean," Kevin's father says, still with that conviction in his voice, that familiar, hateful, imperturbable conviction that what he says, however stupid, is what matters, "is that you're going to meet girls who might as well be named Squeaky."

"Whatever that means."

"When what you need is a Becky. One fair enough to freckle across her nice straight nose."

"Dad."

"Do they make Beckys anymore?"

"My plane. That's its number."

The people lugging babies edge toward the front of the crowd, as does the guy on crutches. Earlier, in line, Kevin and his dad observed a guard going over each crutch with a metal detector. Next was a kid in a wheelchair. The wheelchair, too, came in for a meticulous slow-motion scan, as did the kid's legs, frail thighs discernible under the loose draping of sweatpants. Somebody had tied a silver Mylar balloon to the wheelchair's handle—BON VOYAGE, the innocent touch perfect for a terrorist. Kevin told himself he was sick because he even thought of laughing. He's inherited a sick sense of humor, and he can't just turn it off. He has to learn how to defuse it, how to be more like other people, to feel natural pity, natural empathy, instead of constantly manufacturing these crazy private ironies. The epitome of such an unbearable take on reality stands before him: his father.

"I think it's all Claire now, for girl babies," Kevin's dad is saying. "A generation of girls named Claire is rising right behind you. The Claires are going to straighten things out." Kevin's dad does that frightening thing he does with his hands when he can't afford to want a drink. One hand takes the forefinger of the other and yanks as if to pull it from its socket, a nimble little brutality that has always scared Kevin, not least because his father gives no sign of feeling it. "So," he says. "Hello to my sister."

"Sure."

"Hello to my sister's new husband."

"Sure."

"You'll like him. You will. He's an artist. You wish I was an artist, don't you? Then I could teach you things you'd like knowing."

It has always seemed so inevitable, his father's vagueness, his acidity, his erratic attempts to connect, that Kevin has never bothered to imagine his father as other than he is, but there's no good or kind way of confessing this, so Kevin retreats into the second shrug of their parting. Because it's the second, it seems more dramatic than the first, more pained and adult. At least partly to mitigate this effect, Kevin says, "You taught me a lot."

"Well, that's nice. That's a nice thing to say."

Everything Kevin considers saying next would resonate with defensiveness, and it's torment, trying to get away from his father when his father has such complicated ways of keeping him.

His father says, "No, I know, you need an Andrea."

Kevin shoots him the dogged, determinedly mild expression that occasionally reverses their positions, making Kevin the parent, his dad the kid who's not catching on. "Andrea is my stepcousin's name, remember?"

"Stepcousin. You have such an elaborate way of keeping

track. I guess you need an elaborate way. God knows we've
done enough to confuse you. Stepmother; new half sister;
stepcousin, right, excuse me; *desaparecida* mom."

"Don't say that about her. It's not funny."

"She could write you a letter. When did she last write you
a letter, Kev?"

Kevin's mother has been gone for nearly a year. For a
moment her absence is very specific, and located between them,
where it exerts a ghostly pressure toward greater estrangement
until Kevin says, "That's me. They're calling my plane,
O.K.?"

"You're really going to be gone. I can't believe how this
feels. Listen, look, forget what I said about girls. Forget this
conversation took place. I'm just jealous. I just wish I could
go with you."

"Leaving Caro alone."

"I'd come back."

"I'm not sure you get to tell me this stuff," Kevin says.
"I'm not sure other dads do."

"So you want a normal dad."

"Yeah."

"Break it to me gently."

It's one of their only reliable lines, an old, fond line they
can resort to in real emergencies, and it lets them separate at
last, his father standing back forlorn, Kevin shouldering his
pack and fitting himself into the jam of people waiting for the
attendant to flick through their tickets, tear off a piece, and
hand it back. In one of Kevin's jacket pockets the Sony Walkman rides in its tangle of cord, its earphones a pair of mosquitoes singing to the points of his collarbone. He listens in on
the conversations around him, in case, as he always half expects
in crowds, there are any oblique messages for him.

"—never remember to. An evolving sales force—"

"—won't fly anymore, but takes the train, after—"

"—what she wants. He doesn't say anything. He doesn't answer, and then he goes, he goes, 'Tick tock.' "

This last is so cruel Kevin corks his ears with the Fine Young Cannibals. *She drives me crazy.* On impulse, Kevin wheels to mouth to his father, over the heads of the crowd, *You drive me crazy,* but his father is gone.

In his window seat, before they leave the ground, Kevin begins the game in which you list facts about yourself. The facts have to be habits you know you have, or ways you are, true things, but not things you've ever particularly thought about before, and not obvious things, like the color of your eyes—in Kevin's case the same as his father's, brown, but his father's don't look good because drinkers' eyes don't, and his dad's are growing a welter of fine lines around them. *Welter,* Kevin thinks, for confused. A confusion of fine lines around his father's eyes. Kevin needs to get centered, and there is the game, which his mother invented without naming, just a game, their game, a mother-and-son thing. Fact: Kevin can't stand people who record Vivaldi before the beep on their answering machine. It tempts him to leave something angry but hardly audible, hitting clearly only key phrases: "ding," "BMW," "lawyer," "as soon as possible at 753-4—." Fact: he forgets the minor, necessary tasks his tired stepmother assigns him. He forgets to sort the trash for recycling, yet he spends hours hammering flat and then snipping the tin of old Medaglia d'Oro cans into a mobile for the baby, until ringmaster, bears, horses, dogs, and monkeys, red, white, and green, dip and spin on lengths of transparent fishing line suspended from branches of cholla cactus. She thought it was funny, she thought it was beautiful, but she still minded about the trash. Fact: he's a deceiver. It's in another black-leather pocket, the folded airmail envelope, the secret *Dear Kev,* the *I wonder how you are,* the detailed news he didn't want his dad to get even a whiff of, not because of anything special or disturbing but because any word from Kevin's mother, Hannah, makes Kevin's father nostalgic, and Kevin considers this nostalgia a betrayal of Caro. There are things he's learned to keep to himself: he's getting good. The plane is taxiing. The bump into the air is accompanied by a light-headed rush of fear. No, relief. He'd believed his shameless, dismaying father, in a last sad, overzealous stab at intimacy, was going to show up again, was going to accompany him to California as he'd said he wished he could. Fact: Kevin feels a little wasted, the effort of getting away from his dad cost him so much.

The other seats in his row belong to a pair of Japanese businessmen, both wearing pin-striped suits, both working, neither paying any particular attention to Kevin, who finds himself envying something about them—their haircuts, their brotherly likeness to each other, or simply the golden pen of the farther businessman. Kevin is aware that one or both of them would make polite conversation with him if he wanted, and would not appear in the least put out by the interruption, and it might be soothing to be the object of such compulsive diplomacy, but he can't think of a way to begin. Even their silence conveys a kind of delicate, un-American tact. He wonders if they are fathers, and is sure they are. They must have sleek, dreamy wives in Japan, and fat, proper babies who make few demands, not like wrung-out Caro, not like the chapped, scratched, infuriated, squalling Baby from Hell.

In the pocket holding the letter is another secret, a strip of photo-booth pictures of Andrea, who has hair cut in a kind of black wing along either cheekbone and short bangs, plastic dime-store earrings, intense lipstick, and a finely modeled face too small for the glasses she wears, as if a child feeling across the top of her father's dresser had snatched down his specs. Andrea's is a kind of cultivated, slightly screwy chic that would get her killed in Kevin's high school in Española. He wouldn't want the Japanese businessmen to observe the strip, either. In

a way, her beautifully groomed nerdiness is so like theirs that
they would never perceive her as beautiful. Kevin has wanted
something to happen with her since first seeing the pictures.
It's part of the reason he pushed for this trip. He sometimes
catches himself thinking as if this mysterious *something* already
has happened. He has a series of stories—the kind of anecdotes
that have significance only between lovers, but which, between
lovers, are polished to a doting finish—he imagines telling
Andrea, all beginning "The minute I saw you," though
whether this means the minute he saw her pictures or the
minute he actually first sees her, he can't yet know. When this
strip, four almost identical frames of Andrea, fell from the
envelope onto the kitchen table, Kevin knew he was going to
steal it, so he didn't bother reaching across the dirtied cups
and saucers, but waited for his father to hand it to him. His
father did, asking, "Is this what girls do to themselves now?"
Caro had a week's worth of dishes to do, and her kimonoed
back was perfectly readable—resentment, false calm, exclud-
edness—but this was more or less between Kevin and his dad,
and when Kevin didn't answer right away, his dad went on,
"Why is it so funny to be homely? Explain that to me," and
Kevin would almost have liked to. He would have liked trying
to persuade his father that what Andrea was doing was not
only funny, it was art, but the baby began screaming, Caro
gave his father the hotly direct glance that meant *your turn,*
and Kevin's father went. Kevin could hear him, winded by
even so short a climb, on the stairs to the baby's room, a chaos
of wooden Scandinavian toys, rag rug, diaper pail, and the
space heater blowing across tangles of unwashed clothes be-
longing to everyone in the family, so that waves of people-
scented heat strike the rocker Caro uses to nurse in, singing,
aimlessly, the Mockingbird Song. For some reason, dirty
clothes collected there. Caro had had a difficult night, the baby
up at ten, at twelve, four, six, and now, last-straw fashion,

nine o'clock. "She's supposed to start going four hours between feedings. Penelope Leach says," Caro told the sink, and began to cry, from dreary exhaustion, into the dishwater.

Remembering his stepmother's fatigue tires him, and Kevin falls into a kind of nervous sleep, waking only when one of the Japanese men taps him on the shoulder. Right in that face with its grave eyes, Kevin yawns. It's rude, and he's saying, "Sorry, hey, sorry," even as the attendant, leaning in past the twin, precisely cut dark heads, hands Kevin his toy dinner, etiolated salad, lasagna, peas, a roll, and cake daubed with white frosting. The last head of iceberg lettuce in the world will be torn apart for airplane food. The dressing is oily, the lasagna is as runny as bad catsup, but Kevin can't help it, he's starving. The Japanese businessmen eat with a fastidious spearing style, and it embarrasses Kevin that he will never in his life be able to eat that beautifully, not if he takes the thousand flights they've probably logged, not if he spends hundreds of hours in cramped quarters with elegant men. His fork falls from his tray, and he can't think how to retrieve it until finally he lodges his meal tray in his lap, locks the seat-back tray out of the way, apologizes profusely—"Excuse me, I'm sorry, excuse me"—to the man to his left, and bends to search across the gritty carpet of the floor where there is not only his fork but the gold pen, lying near the tip of an immaculate black shoe, which reflects and magnifies the approach of Kevin's hand as, without thinking, he slips the pen up his sleeve, locates his fork, and, even before he sits up again, goes wild with remorse. The Japanese businessmen have noticed nothing. Kevin rearranges his tray, wipes the fork on a napkin printed with the airline's logo, wipes again from a foolish conviction that it isn't clean enough, and feels the pen sliding, a golden, guilty weight, down the inside of his forearm. From there he eases it into a pocket. Fact: he's a thief. It's then that Kevin remembers sometimes thinking of his father as something other than those things his father so plainly was. Kevin used to think of him as a spy. All boys think of their fathers as spies, maybe. It's so clear that the lives they see their fathers leading can't be their only lives.

In late afternoon, after the pilot has drawlingly urged them to consider this airline in their future travel plans, they land at LAX, and neither of the businessmen, latching their brief-cases in sync, appears aware of having lost anything. Their style of meticulous niceness carries, to Kevin, no tint of suspicion, and if, heads discreetly close, they murmur only to each other, that is because it has been evident all along that Kevin likes being left alone.

Since he was small, when she was the only relative he didn't actively dread seeing, Kevin has called her not "Aunt," but "Michelle." She never used to appear without a gift: garish paints he could streak himself with in the bathtub, a satisfyingly lifelike plastic cockroach, the kite like a hawkmoth that still hangs over Kevin's bed. His father, sure Kevin couldn't overhear, once attributed the exquisite rightness of these gifts to his sister's childlessness: only someone without children would think about children so much. That was during Michelle's first marriage. Though she's eight or nine years younger than his dad, age isn't the only reason she looks so much better. No white sugar in Michelle's diet, no history of messy affairs, no lines around her eyes, no confusion in her future. As far as could be told from her letters, Michelle carried off her second wedding with an élan that made Kevin's father's marriage to Caro seem, in retrospect, depressed, quietly last-minute, compromised by its lack of imagination. Michelle even sent a Polaroid of the wedding cake. On its uppermost tier, instead of a toy bride and groom, one champagne glass, lying on its side, spilled out pink babies, while another poured forth Monopoly money. There has been no news of a pregnancy yet, but Michelle seems to enjoy it that with this marriage she has acquired a live-in stepdaughter.

"Andrea couldn't come to the airport," Michelle says, "but she wants you to know how much she's looked forward to this visit," and it has the overbright ring of a total adult lie. "This is it? Only this carryon?" Michelle doesn't try to take the backpack from him, just gives it a pop with her fist. "You forgot you're here for a month."

He could have thought ahead and realized he would now be as tall as she is. "No."

"Black T-shirt, jeans, and Nikes is your uniform." Playing at maternal omniscience. "You brought one other black T-shirt, one other pair of jeans." Her cocky smile: he's half in love.

"Two," he says. "Two more T-shirts."

"How are you on socks?"

"I'm great on socks." Don't ask about Jockey shorts, O.K.? His face is getting hot.

"How's your old man?"

"My—?"

"Father."

Fall back on something that doesn't sound too false. "No sleep," Kevin answers. "Good, except for no sleep." His dad, who commutes fifty miles each way to teach mathematics at a community college, sometimes spends his nights in his office, which would be fine, even sensible, if the burden of night wakings didn't fall, then, entirely on Caro.

"What's the baby like?"

"A monster." Nothing. "No, seriously, a monster." This should sound funnier than it's sounding.

"Then why, in pictures, is she so killer beautiful?"

"A photogenic monster," Kevin says. "That's not impossible. The Japanese have them in movies all the time."

"A baby the size of Godzilla. Psychic size. I get it."

She's following the arrows that will lead them out of here. He follows her with an obedience that makes him nostalgic, it's at once so lagging and so trusting, and she is saying, "Listen, it's probably hard to believe me on this, because what do I know?, but this part, the sleepless insanely hard part, doesn't last very long." She misses a beat before asking, "Did you try to help?"

Awake anyway at two in the morning, his father gone, Caro in her nightgown increasingly rumpled and hoarse, he'd taken his turn in the rocker, he'd even tried the Mockingbird Song, while in his arms the Afterbirth kicked, arched her back, and howled with disillusion that there was such a thing as a rubber nipple. He says, "No. I wasn't good at it. She doesn't like me."

She misses another beat. This something arrhythmic, unpredictable, there and then not there, in their rapport, scares him. She says, unaware she's repeating herself, "We all have, but Andrea's the one who's really looked forward to your coming," and, fact: he can tell when his aunt is lying. She gives it away; she wrinkles her nose as if she can smell it, the very lie she's leading you to believe, and he understands, without understanding why, that Andrea has said she doesn't want to meet him. The sharp drop in his expectations shows as a greater unreality in the vistas of linoleum, in the terminal's rows and rows of empty chairs, and in his own reflection when, not even excusing himself, he ducks into the men's to splash his face with cold water, and of course it is there, because everything has gone so abruptly wrong, that the elegant fiftyish man in the pin-striped suit turns and exposes to Kevin his penis, cupped in a hand, and Kevin can only back away, hearing himself saying, "No, sorry, no, really, no," to the wistfulness, then the absence of wistfulness, and finally the courteously complete lack of recognition in the older man's gaze.

. . .

When they make it to the Santa Monica house, Michelle pauses at patches of twigs and leaves dry as broomstraw to say sadly, "Dying English herb garden," and then, working keys in a series of locks, calls out with a confidence that expects an answer, but the long living room is deserted. "White carpet," she says. "Arrogant, right? Hostile. We bought this place from a doctor. I can't wait to do it over. Lenny says not yet."

"Doesn't he get paint on it?" Kevin's afraid to set down his backpack. He's afraid to walk into it.

"He doesn't paint here. His studio is over in Venice Beach. He says it's nice to have to leave in the morning, it makes him feel as if he's going to work. You'll have to go over with him. See his work. That's the only way to get to know Lenny. It makes me feel so on-the-surface sometimes."

"So—what?"

"Anyone can know me just by knowing me." She gives him the amused, confiding smile he'd already do anything for. "No secrets," she says. "No paintings to have to go see."

Their things seem so serenely unused, like a composition in a showroom, that it dawns on Kevin at last that she is, or they are, rich, as if he thought her BMW was borrowed, or a fluke. He recognizes a cowhide-and-chrome Mies van der Rohe recliner and a plate, bracketed to the distressed plaster wall, with that lopsided jubilation of Picasso's. In this showroom, the separate costly pieces commune only with themselves, repelling human intrusion. Hostile, yes: his clothes are wrong. His hair is wrong. The pen smuggled this far in his pocket is really wrong, marking him as the most unnatural of guests, an enterprising interloper who, because he steals, might steal again here, CDs from behind glass, the precious plate from the wall, the VCR; and this possibility, which only he is aware of, makes him jump when she touches his arm.

"All right? Come on."

In the kitchen, held to the refrigerator by a magnet that
is a miniature plastic taco complete with shreds of lettuce, the
note says only, "At the beach. L. & A." "You think this is
bad," Michelle says, holding out the taco. "They even have
sushi magnets. This means Lenny and Andrea assumed we
were going to get caught in rush hour. I'm sorry."

"It's all right."

"They could have waited. You might have liked the beach
for your first evening."

"Naw. I would have hated the beach."

She laughs; he can make her laugh.

They've ascended three floors, and the roof above them is
broken by skylights, so that the unpartitioned space is stagily
radiant, when she says, "This is where you sleep." This room,
too, is white, except for the glossy, incredible drift of furs
Michelle begins to clear from the bed, shaking her head as if
he's said something critical. She says, "Lenny's been painting
these. No bodies, just the coats—for their 'sensuous suggestion
of presence,' but I guess I like that better than when he was
painting bodies. These are all borrowed. Southern California,
and he can collect this many fur coats just by asking. We have
different friends. I still think it's strange that it's Republicans
who buy art. This is Lenny's," and she's nodding at the room's
other nonwhite element, an enormous square canvas saturated
with arterial red, the paint applied in strokes so violent that
lines of drip show, though its thin blue letters, as stragglingly
elongated as Giacometti figures, are readable, the three letters
in the picture's upper half roughly balanced on the three letters
tilting across the bottom, so that Kevin reads:

PLI

GHT

"I can't stand that painting," Michelle says. She sits on
the edge of the bed, then leans forward until her face rests in

the furs in her lap, her shoulders still. He sits down close
enough that his leg's against hers. Through a gap in the spill
of her hair, he sees her ear, upside down, a small, perfect pearl
lodged in its lobe. He says, "What?" At the nape of her neck
there's a kind of mustache of brief, erect hairs so blond they're
nearly transparent—this almost kills him. She says, "Oh, this
was supposed to be the baby's room."

"Baby?"

"I had a miscarriage last year."

"I'm really sorry."

She says, "O.K., that's enough strangeness for now. Are you
hungry? Yes? Does pâté sound southern California enough for
you? I want you to know you're not where you're used to being."

In the kitchen, at the counter of celadon tile, under the
poster of the Magritte man with sky where his face should be,
Kevin can't eat after all, but not because she was upset, upstairs. He spent much of the last five years, since the divorce,
with his mother. He knows this about women—some
women—that they can just be walking along, thinking about
something else entirely, when, *bam,* whatever it is that is
wrong blindsides them, and the thing to remember with such
women is that whatever it is that is wrong is wrong all the
time, even when they're not showing it. Michelle's wasn't a
particularly spectacular display, though when he considers it,
its timing was odd.

She eats, too: not the pâté she put out for him, but pasta
salad from one of those transparent deli containers, so that he
knows the couple of ounces she's devouring, with a wedge of
crusty French bread, cost her $2.19. When she grins at him,
her lips have a buttered sheen. "I know. We can go to the
beach. There's a one-in-ten-thousand chance we'll run into
them. I'm going to change."

At the hesitation in his stance, which is the houseguest's
reluctance to impose yet another inconvenience on a host, she
says, "You didn't bring a suit?"

"I didn't bring a suit."

"You're coming to California for a month, and you don't pack a suit?"

He shakes his head as if savoring the particular, refined taste of the irony she's venturing. Fact: he intends to mislead her. The suit that Caro chose for him, and made sure he packed, qualifies as genuinely ugly, livid orchids against a fuchsia ground. He can't believe Caro thought he'd wear it, but maybe she attributes to him a larger, grander kind of self-mockery than Kevin's in fact capable of.

"It's only for a walk on the beach," Michelle says. "I guess you're fine in your airplane clothes. No, look, I'll find you something of my husband's." For the first time, he's been "my husband" instead of "Lenny." Is there any significance in that? Kevin isn't sure whether she wants him to come upstairs with her. When she picks up on his confusion, it's with a small smile, rueful acknowledgment that he's still not at ease. She says, "Try the living room. There's Lenny's 'entertainment center.'" He can hear the quotes in her voice; he's relieved she's cheered up enough for renewed mockery. The cantilevered stairs are polished pale wood, and her bare legs disappear upward. The last dainty lift of the tanned left foot from its aerial step strikes his heart. She crosses the ceiling. She seems to wait in the corner, and he guesses that in this long, contemplative quiet, she's trying to decide what of Lenny's will fit him. Then Kevin remembers that she's told him what to do. Out on the white carpet is an island of couch he settles into, hearing her footsteps now overhead, now receding, then the poised silence that is surely her undressing. On the leather under his hand is the remote control, so he blinks the TV on. The picture, mute, is of a baby in a steel-belted radial, and he snaps through the channels until he hits MTV. Finding it is as close as he's come to homesickness, because however far he's got, MTV is exactly the same. He can't put the sound up or

he'll lose the subtle inflections in her passing overhead, but
when her footsteps aim at the stairs, he lets Sinéad O'Connor's
voice soar to cover him—the depth and insanity of his attraction to his aunt. He's about to turn and make a clever
remark—what?—when something cuffs the back of his head
and falls partly over his face. A soft, worn alligator shirt that
was American-flag red, and is now some beautifully faded
shade of in-between. Something else hits his shoulder and
tumbles onto the couch. A pair of Speedo trunks. Something
thumps the wall—a thong, followed by another. Borrowed
clothes, perfect clothes that will change his life.

She tells him, "Our turn to leave them a note," going
through the spiky cluster of pens and blunted pencils in the
ceramic cup, the one bit of domestic haphazardness in the
entire elegant kitchen. As is customary, Kevin's glad to observe, none of the pens works. "Damn." "Hey, here," he says,
and produces from the pocket of his jacket, hanging over a
chair's back, the almost-forgotten Japanese man's golden pen.
She accepts it absentmindedly, says, "You go dress," and gives
him the push that makes him go.

She rakes hair from her face in a gesture he already knows is
automatic, not a symptom of any particular stress, though it's
true she doesn't seem to enjoy driving, and the Pacific Coast
Highway is busy. She handles Lenny's black Jeep—"More of
a beach car than mine"; Lenny and Andrea took Andrea's car—
with a mild impatience that suggests it's a silly rather than a
wonderful toy. Sunlight spanks every polished black inch. He
wonders how the two of them seem to someone seeing them
for the first time. His mother likes guessing about couples. It's
another game he's inherited: his mother likes, in restaurants or
malls, improvising improbably romantic or funny accounts of
nearby men and women. In the black Jeep with his beautiful

aunt, his bare feet braced on the dashboard, which already feels sandy, Kevin wonders if he looks like her lover. The cotton in the small of his back has sweated through, and his hair is wild. There's a secret sexiness in wearing her husband's clothes, an involuntarily erotic touch of the imposter.

She's talking loudly against the hot air gusting through the Jeep's interior. "I think you and I are lucky about traffic." The crush of sparkling cars is moving fast, though an approaching traffic signal goes from green to amber. "On a bad day this drive takes an hour. Andrea and her father are already leaving the beach. Now, or in ten minutes, we're going to pass them. I wonder if they'll notice us." She does a couple of vague waves, with her bare arm, at the oncoming traffic, and, oddly, a horn does beep. "Was that them?" Kevin asks. "I don't know. *You* and *I* are going to the beach for your first time at the Pacific. They can eat a cold supper and wonder where we are." This attention directed at Andrea and her father makes Kevin jealous, but when they find a great parking space and close up the Jeep, her attention is back on him, where he likes it, where he wants it to be, though he wishes it could take some form other than interrogation. Still, he answers as nicely as he can: how his dad waltzes the baby around when she's colicky, which is every evening at six, singing Woody Guthrie songs into her urgent small screwed-up face. How Caro, who's Nicaraguan, has always liked black beans and rice, but now that she's nursing, that's all she wants to cook, which makes her husband merry instead of irritable. ("That's nice," Michelle says.) How Caro rides Kevin about his homework. ("She should," Michelle says.) What his father gave Caro for their last wedding anniversary: a fly-fishing rod with a dozen flies that he tied himself. (Michelle says, "I love it.")

"Walking by the river all the time, Caro thinks she knows where the really big trout are hiding."

"What's the river?"

"The Rio Grande." They're waiting bareheaded on a median strip with traffic cruising past them in a glittering waist-
high wall. A jogger in spandex jounces up and down beside
them, so they make an odd kind of trio. The jogger won't stop
and rest. He's a sixty-something gent with white chest hair as
frothily immobile as an old woman's perm, and he's giving
them—no, Michelle—the eye. Kevin wonders if he looks like
her son, or a friend of her son's, someone who can be ignored
while the mother is flirted with, because the guy appeals to
Michelle's profile: "Wow. This is bad for this time of day.
Usually, in five minutes, I'm across."

She says, "You're getting lots of carbon monoxide."

He says, "You have to weigh the alternatives: what's good
for your heart but can kill you, against doing nothing and
dying anyway."

She says, "What's O.K. to eat but you can't stand, against
what's terrible but you like."

"What destroys the ozone layer, against what keeps gelato
cold."

For the first time since getting off the plane, or maybe in
his life, Kevin is thoroughly irked with his aunt, irritation
hoarsening his voice as he calls to the traffic, "Come on, let
up." It hears him. He catches his aunt's right hand, the jogger
boldly seizing her left, and, the jogger's crimson-and-lime
shorts flashing, his aunt's hair blowing, they run. On the far
sidewalk the camaraderie of having been stuck together deserts
them, and Kevin gives the jogger a good hard stare to deter
him from even thinking of asking her name or for her phone
number.

Running, Kevin cups up some of the Pacific to taste it,
but the salt bitterness is too sharp to swallow, a mouthful of
cold vinegar he spits out. Gulls take off and hang just overhead,
*scree*ing. Fact: he feels as if he's done this before, waves hitting

almost at his knees, his aunt running at his warm shoulder, on the side away from the water, jabbing now and then at the sunglasses riding down her pinkening nose. A wave slops higher than the others. The meringue of foam melts from the sand; the sand has the sudden reflection-lit enticingness of sidewalks after rain; this too evaporates. Kevin swerves to avoid what's left of a sand castle. After stopping to wing a Frisbee back to a waiting boy, she doesn't resume running, but walks, falling farther and farther behind Kevin until he misses her. She has stopped to talk to a man flying a kite. Talking, she scratches a calf with the toes of her other foot, throwing both arms wide when her one-legged balance is threatened, before walking on. She stops again to talk to an old man fishing from a canvas folding chair. She's driving Kevin crazy. A possessive kind of crazy. The black heads and hooked beaks of the lofting gulls are very distinct in the vaporous light: his heart aches in an unprecedented but familiar way. In the Jeep going home, she asks, "How was it?"

"Great. I feel great."

"That's the difference in our ages. I'm exhausted."

"You don't look tired."

"I'm hiding it. Your first evening in California," she says. She stabs a forefinger in the direction of the sun, an amazing stark, staring golden pink, set in paler golds fading through a spectrum of grays to indigo, and she says, "Going. Going. Gone."

In contrast to her high spirits with him—was she really hiding things?—Michelle seems edgy and thwarted in the kitchen with his stepuncle. Lenny juts a hand smartly into the air in front of Kevin's chest, still clad in Lenny's own old shirt, and Kevin shakes it resentfully, critically, curiously, hoping none of these emotions inflects the handshake. When it's done, it's as if it never happened, like any number of things Kevin thinks of as male rituals, and Lenny says to Michelle, "Andrea disappeared into her room as soon as we got home. Sorry."

"It's not your fault."

"Why, when you say 'It's not your fault,' does it sound like exactly the opposite?"

"Because you expect an accusation. All right. It is your fault. You have total control over your daughter."

"I think this is a little rude," Lenny says, but he's still not talking to Kevin, though he gives him a corner-of-the-eye glance that feels like some kind of contact. Lenny is the sort of man Kevin's mother sometimes refers to as "beautiful." Kevin is suddenly grateful that his mother has always disliked this kind of man. Neither Kevin nor his father is this kind. Not even close—or, to put it another way, the closest Kevin has come is in this actual physical proximity to Lenny. It's taken Kevin five minutes to dislike Lenny with real, teeth-grating dislike, and he warns himself that this is stupid, and to stop it, because Lenny's not dumb and will begin, soon enough, to be aware of it. Lenny says, "I think this is more than a little rude. Jesus, though, she's unpredictable." He addresses Kevin. "Are you unpredictable?"

"No."

"You're sure you're not?"

"What do you want him to say, Lenny? He's predictable. Kevin? He's like clockwork. Nobody Kevin's age appears very knowable to their parents. I think that's part of becoming a separate person. Tell me if I'm wrong."

"She's just—" Lenny begins on Andrea again, but now Michelle, maybe really for the first time getting it that there's something honestly wrong, says, "—just what?"

"Very keyed-up. Very high-strung. I don't know why." Lenny shakes his head.

Michelle says, or asks, "You can't say it's not like her?"

"No, it's like her, only more so."

"So what do you want to do?"

Lenny says, "Do you think you should talk to her?"

Michelle drags the back of her hand across her upper lip

in a curiously unfeminine, oddly provocative gesture. Lenny repeats the question, and Kevin worries for his aunt. Lenny's backing her into a corner, and she says slowly, "I'm not saying no," leaving a brief blank look at her husband for the end of the sentence. In the blankness of the look lies, Kevin knows, the true, secret, between-them *No*.

Lenny says, "Do you think you can talk to her tonight?"

She echoes, "Tonight?"

"Yeah."

"Why tonight?"

"I don't want this to go on any longer," Lenny says. "This behavior. This whatever-it-is."

Their kitchen is far too immaculate to contain this kind of tension. Energy reflects back at them from too many surfaces, and Kevin thinks of Caro's back when she washes dishes at home, and the way his father likes running a hand up under her T-shirt while she's there, not a sexy hand, but an inquisitive hand, a do-you-want-a-back-rub hand, the question so familiar that Caro only laughs, and says, "Later." Adults are always negotiating their ways through mysterious obstacle courses that include pratfalls and trick goals that recede faster and faster the closer you get to them. Kevin knows this, but it's better than the other thing he knows, because of the divorce. Because of the divorce he knows there is such a thing, when two people come apart, as violence. The energy locked in the bond, suddenly released, explodes. Still, his aunt and her husband are nowhere near coming apart. They just, very temporarily, dislike each other.

"We ate at the beach," Lenny says, when Michelle wants to know what he'd like for supper. He says, "That was before this mood struck her. She was fine. See, it's bewildering," and the countenance he turns toward Kevin is, in fact, troubled enough that Kevin finally likes him.

"Kevin, *you* want something to eat," and, yes, he does;

he's ravenous, and besides, he wants to eat something she's
made for him. It delights him that he and Michelle have this
chance to eat alone, Lenny having gone upstairs, his longer
legs and bigger feet doing the disappearing act not half as
prettily as hers. All she makes Kevin, and it's something of a
letdown, is a sandwich, though a nice, heaped one lavished
with mayonnaise; and, idly, inconsequentially, much less tense,
they talk some more. Kevin keeps picking up the restaurant-
style saltshaker on their table, and putting it down a fraction
of an inch nearer her tanned forearm. He can see, finer almost
than salt, very white grains of sand in the down of her forearm,
and this makes him so hotheaded he tries, "Why don't you
want to talk to her?"

"It's not that I don't want to. It's that I'm not good at it."

"You're not?"

"Isn't that what you said about being with the baby? You
know what I mean."

"It's different." He wants to say *You have to get along with
Andrea* but holds his tongue.

"It's a feeling of: I can easily make things worse between
her and me, but there's not much I can do that I'm not already
doing to make them better, so talking to her feels risky."

"How can you make things worse?"

"A hundred ways. I'm a lot of things she's not."

He says, "Like what?"

"Like, oh, blond. Like her father's new wife. Like—I look
a certain way, and she's not sure she likes it, and I'm not sure
it's going to change. Andrea thinks I want things. It's as if
the things I want have to be taken from Andrea. Not taken,
stolen. Stolen is how it feels."

"But you're easy to talk to."

"Thank you." She studies the kitchen vaguely, as if trying
to think what comes next, and he sees—faintly, from a different angle—something of what it might be possible to dislike

in her, and then hates himself for having seen that, because now her gaze is on him. "It helps to have a second opinion." She yawns then, a badly timed and staggering yawn she covers not with a hand but with her raised arm's crook. She's shaking her head apologetically even as the yawn stunningly extends itself. She finishes it off with a sigh, more for comedy than because she wants to sigh. "And here you are," she says. "It's— what?—eleven o'clock for you, right?"

"I'm fine."

"You don't seem even a little tired." She jumps up. "You have everything else you need? Because I'm going up for my 'talk' with Andrea."

Hearing quotes again, he laughs. He wants her sure he's on her side.

He can't tell what happens after the beautiful calves, and the final poignant foot, ascend, because there's silence, or what passes for silence in so oddly acoustic a house. Out of inertia, but also because if he climbs to his—the top—floor he won't be able to hear anything of them at all, he settles into the living room's couch, clicking off the last lamp so that the space feels less intimidating and more private, and he wonders what is happening for at least an hour before it occurs to him that Michelle's not going to come back down and tell him about it. He sits up; heat rushes to his face, his embarrassment's so absurd. "Fool," he says very softly to himself, "idiot. Fool," realizing he's come across his father, late, very late on certain nights in their kitchen, and his father was reciting the same list with the same vehemence, as softly or more softly, and far more ominously to Kevin's child's ear. He'd certainly never asked his father what his father meant by what he was saying. No, that could be guessed. That part was so easy it didn't take a son. Any stranger—say, someone spending his first night in their house as Kevin's spending his first night here—would know at least one reason Kevin's father could rightfully accuse himself of being a fool. Drinking, he's transparent. Kevin humors his dad at those moments when his dad seems to need Kevin not to know what he's known his whole life. Kevin can't think why he's done this, except that his father appeared so crude and desperate that Kevin wanted to cover for him, and the original, generous pretense had required further, more elaborate deceptions on Kevin's part, until he seemed utterly unaware that his father drank. Kevin is delighted to be not under his father's roof but in a place where he has no responsibilities, where he can't catch the innuendo, where he doesn't really know what's going on.

Sleepily, eyes almost closed, he's back to MTV when someone comes down the stairs behind him—that pat-slap of bare feet, and then a voice, not the voice he wants, says, "This is the only TV in the house."

He sits up.

She says more softly, "Sorry. Did I wake you up? This is the only TV in the house."

Not only barefoot but bare-legged, in a heavy long-sleeved sweatshirt, her arms crossed, the sleeves pulled down over her hands so that, really, the sleeves are crossed, tight to her chest, her face familiar to him with its nerd black-plastic glasses cockeyed, her hair tinted a reddish shade of purple and peaking in a kind of cowlick falling over her left eyebrow, her fine freckles doubled by the hours at the beach, and he says, "Andrea?"

"Yeah." To his surprise, she sticks out a hand just as her father did—that fast, that nonchalantly; appreciating the weirdness of being stepcousins, they shake. He likes her hand. It's a small, sane hand, capable, ringless, very light and restive, and he doesn't possess it long, not a second longer than he held her father's. He can see, under the tortured oddity of her hair and the Clark Kents, her father's beauty made delicate, and eighteen years old. She says, "So: do you hate them already?"

"Hate them?"

"I guess I shouldn't ask you that. She's your mother's sister?" He shakes his head. "Your father's sister. Oh. She's your aunt. You love your aunt."

He says, trying for the right tone, "I love my aunt."

"Great. That makes all the men under this roof. Great. I don't care. I can see why."

"You can?" This is a little mean, and she looks suddenly as if she wants to laugh, but they drop it. She doesn't come around to Kevin's side of the sofa, but stands at its back, her hands resting just to the left of his left shoulder, so that he can feel the sofa take the weight she rests on it. The television splashes light around the room. From the corner of his eye he sees her chin, then the wing of her nose, randomly illumined, and he feels as if he's taking in her face in pieces, and that he's never observed anyone more distinctly, and that she is who he was waiting for. She was who he wanted to love, and seeing her he can, though it has the faint anticlimactic taste of a prepared-for pleasure, and is nothing like loving her step-mother. Kevin's wondering if she's ever going to come around to the front of the sofa when a kind of creaking begins overhead, its rhythm, the thudding, the brief lulls ended by resumed and escalating creaking, immediately identifiable.

Andrea says, " 'Making the baby.' " She has quotes in her voice, too, but he likes her for them. Something had to be said of those sounds. What else could be? He is studying her more directly when a flare of light catches her just right, and he sees that she's leaning on a hand whose fingers are crossed. Fact: he's in love.

He's in love. This time he is.

James Was Here

It gets James out of bed in the barely-there light: he's going to carry a gun. He can remember, in a dream, careening down a red-dirt road with the grass on both sides on fire—*Dream? Nightmare, James* (in Gwen's voice, which he still uses for talking to himself; no use wondering when that will change). *Nightmare,* he agrees, and detailed down to the oily wobble in the air over the flaring, vanishing grass, the ash wafting into the pickup cab, *ss*ting tiny holes in his sleeve. Still, it's hard to blame a dream for craziness persisting once he's more or less awake, more or less himself, gazing at himself, the bathroom radiator cold as stone, radiating distilled nightlong cold like a stone. He runs an estimating hand over his face. He hugs himself, breathing his tensed arms up and down and feeling his heart beat. His reflection gazes back—not for the first time, disenchanted, but in danger now of giving way to a darker response, to despair that could flash backward and forward through his life and find no hope, none, for James.

In the bedroom he asks aloud, "This is what you want?," trying to cook a little warmth into the gun with his two hands—it's that small, his hands fold around it, clamshell, pearl—but its iciness is radiant against the small of his back, the barrel nosed down into the waistband of his Levi's, and he keeps imagining his vertebrae as complex vapor in an X ray, the bullet a malign black smudge. *Smudge* because, in flesh, it would wear the aura of its own fragments. James the X-ray tech, one of his many doomed jobs, strapped a fighting, wincing kid to a papoose board, the kid howling for Mom, and the kid's pictures came back with numerous greenstick fractures in various stages of healing plus that night's broken collarbone. Unbuckling the kid, leaning in to be heard over his crying, James said, "I can talk to her." *Mom* was waiting in the hallway, having a smoke. James took the cigarette from her fingers, ground it out, and told her startled gaze, "You can't touch him again like that ever. Hear me?" Yes, she nodded. James caught her jaw between his palms. His thumbs pushed her lower lip slightly upward; she gave it a helpless lick that inadvertently wet his thumbs, and she was listening, she was listening but she told anyway. "I've been wanting to do this," his supervisor said, and fired James. The small of the back doesn't gooseflesh at the gun's cold, though the nape of the neck is all rubbed-wrong, prickling suspense. The body makes unexpected connections, and is honest. *It's* afraid for *him.*

He tries the gun in his old leather jacket: a fit—he can
slip his hand in, close it around the grip, and the leather blunts
the shape enough that it could be his fist, jammed down hard,
James in a mood. With his left fist in his left pocket for
symmetry, and by keeping his shoulders conscientiously even,
he can make this work, though the composition overall is a
little aggrieved or aggressive, maybe—impatient, but people
have compelling reasons for not looking hard at impatient,
unshaven, and mysteriously pissed-off, the kind of passerby
his father used to call *Going nowhere fast* before ruffling James's
hair to mean *Not you, never you.* They'd conducted a steady,
furtive trade in reassurance, that long-ago father and son, but
James failed his part, leaving his father unconsoled, troubled
by troubles over James's head, while James himself intuited
from the nature and vehemence of his father's reassurance where
his father's fears for him lay, exactly. James gets closer to the
closet-door mirror, wondering if this can be true, that someone
(that he) can carry a gun and not have it scream *gun!* The
jacket's hang is handsome with innocence. The cast of his
cheekbone is grave, when James tries a three-quarter profile;
his eyes are lit. He thinks wildly, *I look good.*

Sanity lies in sliding the gun right back onto the closet
shelf where it goes, and to give sanity a chance James prowls his
apartment—every radiator cold; he hates the cold—picking up
at random. His last radiator conversation with Silva ended
with Silva's nonchalant "I'll get to it when I get to it." James
makes coffee and clicks off the kitchen fluorescence to tilt back
in his chair, the jacket over the chair's back, the gun weighing
in with a plumb bob's unwearying love of *down, down, down.*
James might as well be in a canyon. It's the same question of
following not the sunrise but slow secondary dramas. Across
the vague wall of the building opposite, a wedge of Mexican
pink advances, streamerlike shadows unrolling from flaws in
the stucco, crude and slapdash, like so much else about this

place. In the pink wall is the second-story window that, across the elevator-shaft-shaped courtyard bottoming out in rabbitbrush and trash, mirrors his, even to its kitchen table. Too early for the Wide World of Four-Year-Olds, the red-haired single mother feeding her twins. James would love her for her composure alone. She doesn't let the twins throw her, and often enough she's smiled across at James. She can't smile long because the twins don't let her; they know when her attention's elsewhere. Counting other reasons to love her, James can list the fact that she's still smiling when she turns to her kids again, her habit of T-shirts for nightgowns, and the geraniums rampant on her landing when nobody else bothers with more than a parched rush doormat, if that. They've talked brightly in passing—the weather, the rent—without acknowledging that they recognize each other from these windows. James supposes there are rules for being each other's views, and that bright evasiveness is the right style. The twins are redheads, too, which makes the movie they star in a comedy. James is going to wake up one morning over there, in her little bedroom. He's going to deal with her twins at that kitchen table, a stranger relieved of all sadness during the night, grinning, bare-chested, mysteriously at ease, *You kids give your mom a break.* He'll find the Cheerios and pour the milk and let her sleep.

Twenty minutes pass without her T-shirt ghosting across that window, twenty minutes in which he can't persuade himself out of carrying the gun—for no reason, purely to see how it feels, does that make the whim less insane? Moving in here he fell into a routine in which there are tiny checks to the headlong blues, minor consolations to the general mercilessness, all day long, and that's the routine he needs today, checks and consolations built in, little risk of anger and no spur-of-the-moment decisions. He's not brilliant at the spur of the moment. Not necessarily bad, but not brilliant, not good enough to go carrying a gun while improvising. This has to be a day like any other, then. A rule, a measure of sanity, some peace of mind going in.

The gun was Theresa's, a gift from him to her because he was often gone. The gun-store clerk, resting the .32 on the blunt-needled rubber mat, promised, "Women think this is pretty." *Pretty,* gleaming, fine-proportioned, a very blue black, irresistible to hold; when sniffed, neutral cold never-used machine. During the divorce Theresa told him "Take it," she couldn't forget it was in the house, so James keeps it, loaded, on the high closet shelf that otherwise holds, for weird camouflage, dozens of pairs of old-man shoes, the bequest of some tenant vanished or dead, so alone in the world nobody came to collect his shoes. James imagines him sometimes, one of those neat-shirted, gaunt old men, what hair he had left slicked like a beau's, a fragile walker, careful street-crosser, James himself in forty more years of not getting life right.

He yearns for a cigarette, dry essence of clearheadedness. Half a pack, tucked behind a sofa cushion, has bided its time until this emergency, and if he's going to respect the rule of ordinariness, James has to get out of there now. In the parking lot he flirts with two girls, roommates, just climbing into a new Rabbit for the commute to Los Alamos, where they get kitted out like astronauts and, with giant gloves wedged through holes in glass, manipulate flasks of radioactive tinctures. They agree it is a gray day. For the first time he can recall, James is awkwardly aware of what is in fact old habit, keeping his hands deep in his pockets. It is gray, cold enough to justify the jacket, going to rain, which they agree they need.

"We need it." One girl.

"*Yeah,* we need it." James.

"We really need it." The other girl.

James thinks how, if any of them neglected to voice the need for rain, that omission would seem almost violent, a breach.

The waitress has been inspired by Madonna to gild her hair and forget the roots. James likes her, eyes gone very dark because of the stricken hair and her ears harrowingly pierced, though none of these Spanish girls go as far as crucifixes for earrings. Her gold cross, the genuine demure item, rides the pulse at the base of her throat. Harry doesn't make them wear waitress uniforms, and James is glad not to be approached by a jaded little rayon dress every morning. In spite of her destroyed hair, Tina dresses shy. She dresses like the baby sister of five older brothers, which she is. She's got to walk past at least a couple of brothers before she ever makes it out the door. She's in a huge hooded sweatshirt that hangs so far it leaves the merest margin of skirt, black long johns shrunk to skinny leggings with a hole for one knee, and a boy's high-top sneakers. A Band-Aid swathes her thumb except for the flashy red jackknife of the nail.

He says, "Hey, your thumb."

She says, "I know," tired of the story.

"How's your little girl?"

She knows he has a little girl he has every-other-weekend custody of, so this strands them safely on the narrow ledge of what they have in common. "Sick. Running a little fever. But"—tilting her coffeepot-heavy wrist to read her watch, an assured gesture sending a single ring melting across oily black—"I'm going back there on my break, which is soon."

"Come on, Tina, you left her? Or is one of your brothers there?"

"No, everybody's at work."

"You can't do that. Let me talk to Harry."

"No, listen, last night I got *The Little Mermaid,* and she wanted my nightgown so she's in my nightgown, and she's got her pig, and she's so into *Little Mermaid* it will make no difference when I walk in the door."

"Pig?"

Tina does a brief cradling, rocking motion, kid's cheek to ratty stuffed animal, very pretty, rings washing across coffee. Tina whispers. "She asked me; I said a great name for a pig was Harry."

"Harry needs to remember you have a kid."

"He's too mean to remember that." She says, "No, listen, *Little Mermaid?* 'S a good movie, really. Everything Ariel says?, she says right along with her. Plus I wrote the number here on the back of her hand in case she thinks she needs me." Tina displays her thumb, a hostage to distract him. "Cooking for my brothers. I chop right up the chili into my thumb. *Wow,* it burns. My brothers come blamming into the kitchen."

"You're cooking when you're tired. When you're tired's when you hurt yourself."

She laughs. "Tell me when I'm not tired."

"You have to be more aggressive. Ask Harry for the day off when your kid is sick."

"Don't you remember being tucked in dreamy, with a fever? How it wasn't so bad? Didn't your mother ever have to leave you like that?"

"You don't want to take any lessons from my mother." He slides a fist toward the table edge her hip leans into. "And me? What if I think I need you?" If he pushed his fist any farther, it would rest against marginal black skirt, girl's hipbone, girl. Intimately, girl. When she shifts her weight to her other leg, it distances her easily and doesn't accuse him.

"Something happened: you've been in here a lot of mornings and not needed my number."

"I happened. I'm awake."

She's amused. "Awake." She doubts it; she likes it. The
home dye-job on her long johns is crudely, excessively black,
and the exposed knee has the candid availability of an egg. He
tells her, "I'm in love with your knee."

She says "Thank you" absently, then "You broke up with
somebody," the pounce in her voice small-scale, decisive insight. Five brothers: she must often confront wayward moods,
inexplicable reversals, and either she figures these out on her
own, or her brothers remain mysteries. She's learned to trust
herself. It gives her a nice confidence. When she tries her
conclusion as a question, it's for politeness's sake. "You broke
up with somebody?"

This isn't their usual conversation, which is how she can
know him and not know about the end of the world. He says
disarmingly, straightaway, "Right."

Tina says, "I'm getting married."

"Tina—shit—again? What for?" She takes this for rudeness, so he mends his ways with the story of his life. "I was
married. To my little girl's mother. We're still friends. I
almost got married again, not that long ago, either, but—
right, you're right, we broke up, I still don't know what hit
me."

This much truth renders them mute until she lights on
"More coffee? I should look like I'm working."

Is she pleased this exchange petered out without a really
bad moment between them? She pours. It's in her lowered
eyelids that she's pleased.

Five, a number of brothers that had to make or break her.
They live, she's told James, in a couple of trailers on land they
inherited when their folks died in a car crash. Strictly speaking,
the six of them own a small piece of land each. If they divided
it up, none of them would actually own enough land to put a
trailer on—thus, togetherness. She's told James of ex-girl-
friends driving out late at night to discover that only Tina will
come to the door or sit at the kitchen table with them while

they cry. She's told James she's learned from experience not to wake any of her brothers, no matter how the girlfriends plead. None of her brothers knows how to be any consolation, Tina says.

James reads want ads, finding nothing worth circling. He got his contractor's license last spring, but it hasn't meant what he'd hoped it would mean, constant work. Mist blossoms on the window over his cup, erased by glassy cold when he lifts the cup, his freshened coffee hot as fever, the glass alive with reflections, a brilliant, shifty collage of outside and in— the levitated salt and pepper shakers suspended over a distant mesa, a shard of James's forehead with little rivers coursing down it. A radio-tower signal blinks interestingly from within the salt. Tina stops at his table as she's leaving. "Raining good, huh?"

"It needs to keep raining, not drift off somewhere else."

"I know I'm supposed to hope for that, but it messes up our road. You didn't eat much." She takes his plate, though it's another trip to the kitchen for her, and the dollar from under the saltshaker.

"Tell your little girl 'Feel better' from me, O.K.?"

"If she knew who you were."

"You never mention me?" He's sounded hurt; he tries to invest less in "Never?" She can't rescue him. "But I'm in your life every morning. Right here every morning. If I wasn't, you'd miss me."

She handles this as five brothers have taught her to, winsomely, giving him time to get it together. "Are you going to be gone?"

He's not her responsibility, so why does it take his shaking his head *No* to free her of this conversation?

"Then I won't miss you." She smiles at him steadily, her smile losing certainty because she wants to be, then is, out of there.

James sticks around until her old Camaro, juiced up by

one of the brothers in celebration of a little sister's beauty, jars across the potholed parking lot. Its taillights burn in brief reckoning, it cuts across the Santa Fe–ward traffic, and she's tucked the Camaro between two semis in the northbound frenzy, the second eighteen-wheeler leaning vengefully on his horn, James whistling under his breath, the taillights that are *Tina* shut off from view and carried away. Leaning on his elbows he tries the funnies, but without her this could be anywhere, spread newspapers and smeared plates, or nowhere, with nowhere's neon-ringed clock and the apocalyptic desert sunsets that appear paint-by-number but aren't, nowhere's Muzak, nowhere's regulars, nowhere's truckers whose brooding gazes have traded an external, verifiable broken yellow line for an inner one, stroke of yellow, tick of black, stroke of yellow, real enough to undulate, climb hills, pass through woods. James stands, and the gun slides downward like a bolt. To the hand that seeks it out it's reality, chill and shapely, persistent, intelligently receiving the hand that closes around it, offering a wonderful handhold. James walks a self-conscious, self-fearful walk toward the register, negotiating with himself for reasonableness. After such long dislike, it's a pleasure to carry a threat toward Harry, and he doesn't want this to be too much of a good thing, he doesn't want to go astray. A heavy-hipped waitress, standing out of James's way, rests against a table, and her bottom, faced toward James, is so humanly beautiful it calms him, it lets him say to himself, *This is crazy.* Behind the glass counter, big slabs of breast under a completely buttoned-up cowboy shirt, straw-pale hair oiled to keep to his scalp, the half-moons for close reading etched in his bifocal lenses, is Harry, Harry taking note of James, James choosing two mints from the dish, Harry telling James, "Nickel each."

James, incredulous: "Can't be."

"It's sad."

James says, "Is Tina going to keep working after she's married?"

"Has she told me? I warned her I need some notice, too."

On the spur of the moment James says, "A pack of Marlboros. No. Yeah."

"Which?"

"Give me the cigarettes."

Harry receives two more dollars, then refigures the constellation of James's change on glass, his left hand sheltering the coins he's entitled to. James loathes that hand, balanced feyly on its fingertips like some big raw-red crab, its digits cumbered by turquoise, its back turbulently veined. He loathes that hand as if Harry lives in that hand and the peaceably mean bulk straining at the cowboy shirt, the wattled, corded throat, are an afterthought, and the hand alone true Harry. *Wow*, James thinks, Tina's word, Tina's tone of startled homage to what it's possible to feel, and then Harry confounds hate. Harry says kindly, "I remember when they were pennies, those mints. Used to steal the pennies, I'm afraid, from my mama's purse."

James tells Harry, "She probably knew."

Harry shakes his head, unself-forgiving, then back to mean, wondering what's keeping James.

James resists opening the pack, feeding himself candy instead. The taste of peppermint pales from his tongue as he drives north for thirty minutes, passing Tina's road without wondering how she is, instead wondering how Gwen is, breaking, so early in the day breaking, his rule that this day can be no different, because he's going to act on that wondering, the oncoming headlights a dazzlement undimmed by rain, he's going to go see, the junipers holding fast with bonsai cleverness to the small eroding hillsides, the arroyos rushing knee-deep and resonant. Even before the rain's over, a high-altitude rainbow fades in, in the northeast, a trembly smear of gold and blue-violet, nothing steady about it, not one of the far-flung, surreally stable rainbows that can stop traffic along this highway after storms. On the dashboard are the small stones his daughter collects, one from each place they go together.

The red dust, with its matte, unnatural dryness, like sodden baby powder's, takes boot prints graphic as the finest
evidence, and James fights the heavy gate closed on its rusted
hinges, securing the lock behind him while his truck idles its
own fog of exhaust. He remembers—not consciously, but up
from below, in reflexes—the shifts and dodges of this skiddy
three-quarters of a mile, the road from last night's dream,
though he wishes he didn't suddenly understand that, or have
to wonder what it means. He can't remember sleeping, only
needing to sleep, only pitching his paperback thriller at the
wall, 3:00 a.m., and, 4:00 a.m., having to get up to get it.
A low-level glitter hangs in the ricegrass, in the chamisa and
black greasewood—drops the size of orange seeds, maybe, but
found out, though clouds ensure the sun's no brighter than a
moon, a big moon rolling in and out of visibility. No Volvo,
no smoke from either chimney, nobody home, and if his rule
for today is broken, it's not smashed into irretrievable pieces
as it would have been if she were home, a risk he ran without
arguing it through with himself, without any counterself urging *James, wait.* That no such counterself roused itself to
contest his impulse is weirdly lonely: he doesn't want to believe
he's alone with the gun. James wanders around the house,
giving the front door a rattle in passing, turning corners for
the clicks of recognition that build toward the five senses' very
favorite consolation, maybe, in the world—being back, being
home again, because this is *it* for James, the one and only
place: whether he likes it or not, he's rejoicing. Small birds
flash up before him, and then with nowhere to go wing around
overhead, hoping he's not staying long, recognizing the unusual, the break in the house's routine of daylong abandonment, dewed foxtails swatting James's knees and slipping apart
in a trail, tamped-down grass behind him, the post-rain fra-
grances manifold and earthy, muddy, grassy, airy. This small
house lives alone on its pale sandstone ridge in such a fastness

of pale, abandoned ridges that the scale of the inhuman is
lunar here—even litter is touching, like litter on the moon,
companionable. James kicks at a tin can rusted to oxblood.
This is Spanish-land-grant land, and the title to this place is
worth *nada*, or they'd have tried buying it. The laundry gusting on the line behind the house is Levi's in five ages of blue,
and at her long-leggedness his heart beats faster. The back
door he rehung to stop snow fanning in across the threshold is
locked, and the key's no longer hidden under the cat's water
dish. James fishes a drowned wasp from the dust-skinned water, favor to a cat he didn't like. If James pauses before what
he does next, it's not so he can think. He's not thinking, he's
more or less riding on the blitheness of compulsion, that
energy, when he tries the latch on a window. The window
grates upward, letting him in. This room resists his intrusion
by a sly warp in its perspective—known, but not from this
angle—by a lack of charity in her brass bed, by the whiteness
of the bed's white quilt he drops his black leather jacket on,
by the conviction in its quiet. He can stop right here, without
having trespassed far at all, barely having got in, but his bowels
cramp subversively, insisting on the matter-of-factly territorial
shit he enjoyed after absences from home, brief times gone on
some job or other. Boot prints lag down the hallway's polished
floor after him, and seated on the toilet James works hard not
to hate himself.

James strips off his T-shirt and gets barefoot to mop, the
hallway's ruddy smear widening and growing abstract, James
warming to the work, restoring the gleam to floorboards she
refinished, sanding off years of scabbed varnish. After serious
effort, the floor's redeemed and shining, and he was never here.
He should go.

He tells himself he's going, but her refrigerator is riches,
white boxes with wire handles, white-paper packages taped in
white, stacked Tupperware with cloudy innards, mineral water

in ranked chill tints. If he eats judiciously from several different boxes, he won't have to empty any of them. In the glare of intensely clean cold, his nipples erect, James eats deftly from boxes he opens carefully, so they'll close perfectly—tomatoes dripping vinaigrette back into their box, slices of rare roast beef, grilled red peppers lank as seaweed but meltingly sweet, lamb curry whose sauce has congealed to a stinging paste, small almost-bitter olives. Eating with his fingers, he's as far from conscience as a wolf.

His first serious chance of finding her, if he's going to try to find her, is at the restaurant around three, in the lull following lunch. If he's unlucky, she'll use the downtime to shop. Her roving perfectionist's progress, rubbing the nap of each peach, checking the gold-leaf eyes of trout for iridescence— can absorb the afternoon. Well, if she didn't obsess about details, she and Dwight (her partner: gay) could hardly hold their own in a town full of restaurants, as Santa Fe is. She can tease buckshot from pheasant, render rose leaves in lustrous chocolate, bargain for venison with local hunters, guys with prison tattoos on their *faces* and a scary delicacy in negotiation. She's good the way you're good if you *love what you do,* if it keeps you up all night some nights, if, other nights, your trivial mistakes loom in your dreams, and her sense of what was wrong with James was that he needed *something to love,* at which it was possible to look into her dark, strict eyes with their strikingly clear whites and laugh; and she would say severely *Besides me.*

Outside the bedroom window he neglected to close, two sparrows start in (she would tell him what kind; lying in bed she could tell one meadowlark from another). Their niches in sage are dry. Naked except for his Levi's, James does what he has no right to do, tucks himself under her quilt, gathering his jacket to himself as a child gathers its blanket, not for comfort exactly but from some sense that the jacket's more dangerous, or maybe only more real, sprawled across the foot of her pretty bed than in his arms. This way, even sleeping, he'll know where it is. He checks the safety—the gun malignly, mechanically black against the linen—and slides the gun back into its pocket. He hugs the jacket and sleeps like a child, parted as completely as a child from *what just happened* and *what's going to happen,* James gone, really gone and not dreaming. When he wakes, he's forgotten where he is, and it takes a strand of Gwen's hair on the pillowcase to orient him. Awareness of being watched brings him entirely awake. Oh: her striped cat has composed itself on the windowsill into a kind of sphinx of accusation. This trick of cats', suggesting reproach and heavenly tolerance at the same time, irks him. He'd like to sleep again, to sleep as he was sleeping, but he'd have to get rid of the cat, and the cat's not leaving as long as it has James's gaze to return; the tension, the refusal to let go first, feels a little like lovers at odds. James hides his face in the crook of an arm and lets Gwen's bed—(he can't leave any trace he was ever here)—be a good place to daydream in. That padded thump is the cat landing on the floor. She finds James. She's upset but willing to listen, to give him a chance. When she asks the reason for this break-in, he says, *I can't stay away. I tried,* and hears, as he would in real life, *You have no choice.* Even in his daydream she says he has no choice. She says bluntly, *I don't need you.* (*Therefore you can't need me* is meant.)

Is it that you don't believe in needing in general, he asked once, *or is it that you don't believe in needing me?* She said, *You're as close as I've come to needing anyone,* and thought that was an answer.

His watch tells him 2:20, which is good. He can try catching her. The last couples are swallowing their last forkfuls; Felipe has only to lean against the wall to encourage them out. In the bathroom James rinses the taste of daytime sleep from his mouth and lets the water run across his face. He could shave with Gwen's razor, but he owes it to her to appear aimless, vagrant, *going nowhere fast,* as borderline as she feared he'd be without her. He closes his eyes for a rest from his reflection, but can't rest long. The gun functions like inspiration, and his reflection's eyes are, right, readably hostile. He protests *This isn't me,* which translates as *All this anger isn't me,* which translates, at the deepest level of self-contemplation, as *I'm a good man,* and at that level (he doesn't know himself any better than this; he can't get any more inward or try for any securer understanding), this avowal is met by doubt. He wills it into clarity—*a good man,* I'm telling you—but it's clouded. Doubt has credibility: well, look at him.

By the time he's sure she won't be able to tell he was in her house, by the time he's gone back through it twice, even remembering to collect the cat and dump it outside before closing the window, his watch says 2:43.

Behind the glass door, Felipe mouths a word that could well be *Shit,* and lets James in. Felipe sits back down at the table where he's copying out the evening's menu, which he'll take down the street to Xerox on costly paper. His handwriting possesses the antique Spanish dashingness with which New Mexico was stolen for the king. He calls while writing, "Gwen. Problem."

Gwen, from the back, "Tell me the kind of problem."

Felipe considers James; James doesn't want to hear the kind; Felipe calls, "Come see."

Gwen calls, "Even in *Jeopardy!* I'd get a category. I can't leave this, F."

Felipe calls, "This needs you, O.K.?"

Needs her.

Her composure, her crossed arms—those could have been predicted; and her narrowed eyes, anticipated in the hundreds of imaginings that haze this acutely actual moment, are no less hurtful because he could have known she'd take no longer than this to wish him gone, James suffering a kind or quality of hurt whose phrasing would ring strange: *She's so herself,* that's what hurts, completely separate, fresh and undiminished, while he is all raw nerves and frank loss, still. She says, "James. Nothing's changed."

He says ruefully, knowing that rue is the saving grace here, "You're sure."

He did that well enough, and it was brief enough, to give her pause, to cause her expression to change to slightly less sure, reason for James to just as slightly push. "If something changed and I were you, I'd listen. I'd give me a chance. I couldn't be so cold."

Cold flirts with overkill. Felipe laughs and tells Gwen, "No? All you have to say is one 'No.' "

To fend off that *No,* James should lift both hands and hold their palms toward Gwen, the body's instinctive representation of innocence, which he can't use because of the gun in his pocket. Inability to make this gesture infuriates him, the just-right response eluding him when he needs all the help he can get. "Give me five minutes, Gwen." Almost a slip of the tongue. Almost *honey. Honey* would have had him out of there fast.

"No?" Felipe tutors her. "Little word: *N. O.* All you need," and it could be this, Felipe's readiness to do James harm if he can, that causes Gwen to relent, if relenting is saying "Say whatever is on your mind, say it, and get out."

"Gwen: Can we be a little private? It's important."

"Important."

"Yeah."

This corner scarcely qualifies as private, but at least Felipe's not in James's face, and James out of Felipe's force field is a lighter-hearted James who might even be good at this. They sit, and Gwen says, "How am I? Fine. That's what people

start with after going from who we were to each other to
who we are now, the kind of fucked-up small talk nobody
can bear, really. If we ran into each other on the street, I
could understand it, maybe, but you're making me talk like
this here. How are you? Don't answer that. I won't tell you
how you look." Then she can't resist. "Like hell." Angry at
him.

He says, "No small talk? I miss you like an arm. A leg. I
can't look good or be good, sleep or eat very well, make sense
of our being apart."

She leans back. Her couple of inches' new distance figures
in her voice, too. "You made nonsense of our being together.
Is how I see it."

"I can change that." He tries to wait longer than he can
actually stand to. "I've been working on myself. I can be
different with you." He waits, but she's handling this with
silence. "I know it can't seem true," he says. "Hearing it like
this, of course you're skeptical."

"Skeptical," she says. "I passed skeptical so long ago.
Skeptical was one of the pleasanter emotions."

"There isn't anybody else, is there?"

"The rights you assume you have, you amaze me." But
answering the question at all, she has to answer, *No, nobody.*
He knows her that well, and she knows he knows.

He says, "I can't live without you. I'm not good at it."

"I could have told you you'd get to that. I could have
written it down and kept the piece of paper with me and
unfolded it for you when you showed up and let you read it
and you'd see: *I can't live without you,* when you know that's a
lie, you can, and you have to. *Saying* that, can you feel what
blackmail it is?" She veers away from him without leaving her
chair, by uncrossing and recrossing her long legs.

He says, "I mean *live* like understand why I'm getting out
of bed in the morning, *live* like knowing why I'm here, like

there being this great reason, you, for dealing with how very
fucked-up the world is, being able to deal with it, a motive
for getting through the day, and you know that, you know
telling you this isn't blackmail, it's love."

"Love," She runs a finger around the neck of her T-shirt
so the mole under her collarbone shows. Seeing him following
her gesture she turns it into a yank, the T-shirt's neck a noose.
She says, "Know what I read in the paper? They did this study
of men and women to see whether lovers can recognize each
other. Blindfolded, whether they can find their lovers in a
same-sex lineup, by touch."

"You're telling me this because?"

"Because a blindfolded woman can find her lover, but a
blindfolded man can't."

"Look, Gwen, blindfolded, I'd have a hundred ways of
knowing you. You're wrong. You couldn't find me. You're so
wrong it hurts."

Felipe's pen pauses so he can examine them, or not them,
Gwen, her profile to James, the long, slightly upturned nose,
the eye intelligently bracketed by crow's-feet, the ear unevenly
hidden by her short hair. Felipe perceives some signal James
can't, and resumes his scratching, radiating irritation, and, as
if in response to that irritation, Gwen smoothes and smoothes
a table napkin.

James tries a more neutral topic. "How's Juan?" Juan,
Dwight's lover, was in the hospital, the last James heard.

"Home, but hurting. They even say this could be the
week. James, it's awful. Dwight's with him a lot."

James, it's awful—her resistance rubbed away to show
plaintive old affection and dependence; he says, "That's good.
Dwight has to be. Hard on you, though."

"Dwight found a new guy, a friend of a friend, to help for
now."

"Is he any good?"

"Only all right. It gets awkward, because so much of how I work needs Dwight for its other half. It's having to discuss what Dwight would automatically know. This is selfish, sick of me, but I can't help wondering if—, if—, how long before Dwight can come back?"

"Not sick. Natural. You know it's natural." James says, "Can I come for you after work?"

"James: one five-minute conversation, and it's filled with trouble, and you, only you, could think we're seeing each other again. We're not. We can't. You know what this was, James? This was you getting what you wanted."

At the door he says, "See you," and she says, with beautiful weariness, "No," and waits while Felipe locks up, Felipe glad James is gone, and James *is* gone, he's almost to the street before he turns to run back up the stairs. When he opens the door again, Felipe's expression is grounded like an actor's in powerful, recollected wonder, not genuine but dramatic. "What?"

James writes on a receipt with a stub of carpenter's pencil. *I'll come back. We're not finished talking. J.*

Felipe reads. "She said the N-word, James. About time."

"None of your business, Felipe. You're not even close enough to be a bystander to Gwen and me. I gave you a message, you give the message to her."

Felipe tears the scrap apart and lets it confetti the industrial carpet. James's chemistry thinks it's Christmas and he's awake before anybody else in the house, James alone knowing it's really Christmas. "Felipe, don't you hate this place? Hate yourself?"

"Myself?"

"Tourists eating here spend more in one night than you make in two weeks, right?"

Felipe rests a hand on James's jacketed shoulder. The hand is gentler than seems possible, given Felipe's eyes, unbelievably gentle, and James backs away until Felipe can close the door between them. Felipe locks it with aggressive grace and no wasted motion. With a last grave look of complete mutual incomprehension, they part. James understands it was only luck that Felipe was gentle.

As James passes a tall girl, she raps on a shop window, as if wanting in, but not really—he discovers when he stops behind her—really indicating to her also-lanky girlfriend the amber bracelet that's alone, in the window, in being valuable. The two women are a pair of pretty smiles switched on for James. That kind of instant wattage, it's Texan. He tires himself entertaining them, not long but charmingly, playing the native. He guesses what their visit has been, and how insecure they feel, tramping around in furs and cowboy boots. All tourists carry with them the premonition of mockery. James teases them into feeling briefly at home.

By the time the clerk, in her sixties and soft-spoken, fetches the bracelet for James, the tall girls are gone. Neither proved bold enough to follow James into the shop. James likes the amber's resinous satiny lack of resistance to handling, and the darkness variously shading the deep yellow beads. Their sensuousness conjures for James the marbles he collected as a kid—the sensational rattling of marbles centrifugally swilled and popping in an old coffee can. The best gifts have this doubleness. The amber can mean marbles to James, and, to Gwen, love after doing without, smarter love, love he'll do nothing to harm. He's daydreaming; he hasn't got this kind of cash, and can't recall paying his last credit-card bill. It's funny considering the older woman as witness, and then considering himself considering—Didn't he just skip several steps? Why does he feel so at ease? She could go either of two ways—hyped-up frailty, suddenly old on the witness stand; or

a sage calm, giving the accused a level gaze over the rims of
her bifocals. She would tell the courtroom she liked him. She
does like him. When he rests against it, the counter's struck
by the muted, leather-hidden thud of the gun his hand is
closed possessively around, and when she studies him—he was
right; he gets a due severity over the specs—he smiles as if
apologizing for bumping a hip into the glass, a man, after all,
in this jeweled, feminine, musical environment, a man trying
to do the right thing, and she smiles and goes back to straight-
ening a row of bracelets on a severed arm of black plaster. He
says, "I want this. Can you wrap it?" and skates his surely
useless card across. What he wants is to get closer to robbery
without committing himself completely.

She's pleased for him. "It's very special."

"I'm—we're—celebrating."

"Good!" She feeds his Visa to a machine and gift-wraps
skillfully, pleating gold foil into fine corners as if making a
tiny bed, and he's about to take the small new-minted box
when she says, "Oh, my." He says, "Oh, my," quoting her
confusion as much as her phrase, and she says, "It's *no*-ing your
card."

"It is?"

"Definitely is." She's flushed and sorry and, from empathy,
humiliated. She'd love to salvage the situation—James's ego,
for some reason, is most dearly her concern, which means he
can't do, can't carry off, what he was only half thinking of
trying anyway. Can't do that to her. He says, struck, "This
has never happened to me before."

She grieves: "Your celebration!" She understood well before
this that he has no cash on him, or they would have had a
graceful way out. The bell on the door jars and the clerk says,
"What I can do is hold it for you. Under the counter. Until
you can come back," and James says, "I'm not going to be
back," and walks out past a middle-aged guy, suit and tie and
the right to the clerk's immediate attention.

. . .

Theresa's in an old sweatshirt of his. He's sure, because of her judicious lean around the door, that except for his UNM sweatshirt she's in her underwear. He says "Honey?" on an interrogative note of reassurance. She says "Hi" hoarsely, rising on the balls of her bare feet before kissing him, her mouth harshly chapped and her breath eucalyptus-medicinal. He says, "Sick, huh?"

"I was sleeping. Cindy's home too."

"Is she pretty sick?"

"Not so bad today. She had it first, as usual, and I kid myself I'm not going to get it. What are you doing here? This isn't one of your days."

"I was in town."

Her "Oh" comes in the small voice that means she thinks he was seeing Gwen, and he doesn't know how to disillusion her. He suffers the bone-marrow bleakness that comes of hurting Theresa so fast, without meaning to. She long ago adopted this attitude of deference toward Gwen, and he never did what he needed to do—talk Theresa out of it, leave her sure of herself and unashamed and able to hold her own. That's what his primary sense of Theresa is, even now: he wishes she could hold her own.

She says, "Could you get the papers?"

He has to stoop for three *New Mexicans*. "Jeez, Theresa."

"I'm sick."

"The neighbor kids are going to start making up stories about this house, like: a crazy woman lives here. Stay away."

"Nope. They trust Cindy to have an O.K. mom, plus none of their moms do much better. Do you know how many houses you can count down before you come to a house with a man in it?" They study the row of tract houses in wan adobe shades and he says, "No, how many?" and she says, "I was just joking. I don't know." Nervously: "Lots."

James's mother would make an amused mouth when she answered the door for his father. James's father would wonder if he could leave James for a while, and she'd ask, "Off on another adventure?" which meant, grown James translates, *Off with another girlfriend?* but *girlfriend* wasn't a word that got spoken. No. James's mother wasn't indifferent to his father's charm. They would both be smoking, his mother and father, committing the identical extravagant courtesy of glancing sideways to exhale; this coincidence would leave them smiling, and James would watch their smoke cat's-paw the farther, upward air, thinning through several shades of hardly there before really being gone. He couldn't look at them. They didn't look at him, either. They sometimes left him there; that didn't mean he was alone. He wasn't sure it was *his house,* but he could go in. He was supposed to go in and supposed to bear his awareness of them, wherever they were. Why think "wherever"? They were upstairs in her room.

James says vaguely, "I wish there were men."

"*You* wish." He recognizes the arc of white latex flying from the sweatshirt's collar down her chest. He can even recall the slip of the brush. They were painting the ceiling of Cindy's room in this house, just bought, and when she splattered him, they did the Coke-commercial thing, painting each other's noses white, et cetera, in love. Years ago. She wipes her nose on her sleeve and he says "Jeez" again, annoyed, and she laughs and leads him inside, his carrying the gun into this house yet another kind of violence, violence without the least degree of justification and no quickening of interest—boredom, rather, the monotony of having to keep a secret, the small, oppressive difficulty of recollecting just what can't be said. He wanders through the living room in his black-leather jacket. She calls from the kitchen, "You can have coffee or tea. I'm making tea for me."

She's resting against the stove. He says, "You go back to

bed," and she yawns. Her forehead sweats against the hand he holds to it—his left hand, his careful right hand still in with the gun. He says, "I'll make the tea. I'll baby you."

"Baby me? Why?"

"I'll give you a back rub."

"Back rub? Why?"

"Because we should do better. Do better by each other."

She says, "Why are you really here, James?"

"We made this beautiful kid, right?"

"Then you should have been good to me for the last five years, right?"

"Back to bed. The kitchen's cold."

This was critical in tone, and rouses her. "You're not paying the bills in this house anymore. I am."

"But if you're sick, and she's sick, it should be warm. You conserve on the wrong things."

"I'm a hundred and one and she's a hundred and something so we don't mind the cold just now. Thank you for telling me how to live."

"I'm not."

"You came to the door five minutes ago, and you've already pointed out several things I should be doing differently. I saw you think about telling me I shouldn't answer the door like this."

"Well, do you think you should? Do you think it's a great example?"

"She's *asleep* and not having any ex*am*ples right now and who are you to say *examples?*"

"You go back to bed, I make tea for you, I bring you your tea, I give you a back rub, you start to feel better, huh? How's that sound? Maybe I do have some ideas—like you shouldn't come to the door half-naked—but you do O.K. It's me, my fault: I need to take some of it off your shoulders, right?"

She yanks the hem of the sweatshirt down past her panties

and holds it down with a fist, though this means she's in an awkward position when she covers her eyes with her other hand to cry—stricken, fervently ugly crying, each insuck of breath rattling with mucus. He can't put his arms around her, and can't wait her out. He says, "What if you go back to bed, I bring you your tea, I give you your back rub, what if that, huh?" and she uncovers her eyes and kicks. Her bare foot misses his knee and she kicks again and connects with his shin and she pounds on his shoulders, not hard enough to anger him, but she makes herself felt. Because he doesn't back away, it feels sexual, the authority with which she's forced herself against him, focused formidably on him. He says, "Hey. Hey. Hey, don't hurt me," his defense having to do with preventing her finding out about the gun. He keeps his elbows pointed out, chicken-wing fashion, his fists deep in his pockets, leaning his left shoulder toward her to guard his right side. His keeping his hands in his pockets could easily be *I can't hurt you, see?*, a male stratagem she furiously resents, then chooses to be amused by. When she leans into his chest, done, he risks taking his hands out to hold her, setting his chin on the top of her head, his nose to the dour, reproachful scent unwashed hair has, both of them calmer and calmer until she says, "I hate it when you remind me how you *can* be."

"Maybe I could be like that all the time, sometime."

"For somebody else."

They consider this with sadness.

He says, "To bed, O.K.?"

"You're here. What are you doing here? Are you leaving town? You haven't come to say good-bye, have you?"

"I'm not saying good-bye, I'm bringing you tea."

When he does, she sits up in bed, crying again while she drinks her tea, but this crying is private, neither strategic nor caused, or not very directly caused, by James, who can therefore keep her company in it, this almost companionableness of sitting neutrally near her on the bed without touching her. He remembers, unwillingly, the morning he screwed up conclusively: so in love with Gwen he was getting stupider and stupider with Theresa, running flagrant risks, rubbing her nose in it (he sees now), denying everything with such heat he invited the next question, and the next, and the eventual end, which Theresa, for reasons of her own (because she is Theresa), delicately, decisively, almost maternally withheld. He and Gwen had stayed at a really terrible hotel, all they could afford that particular spring night, and even coming into this house and finding Theresa awake at 5:00 a.m. he'd thought he could carry it off, thought she'd make one more covert deal to keep their life the way it was, precariously was. His story, of the truck breaking down near Galisteo, forty miles south, where he'd gone to inspect a job site—his story was fine. Standing, he'd rested his hands on the kitchen table, leaning into it, full of weird confidence that came, maybe, of lovemaking, gazing down at Theresa, and her look had the frank mistrust he'd come to associate with a successful lie; and he would watch that look of mistrust turn startled, then utterly bleak, as she looked from his shirt and back to his ignorant eyes and to his shirt again, so that he glanced down at the cockroach, long as his little finger, clambering from his pocket and then, with apprehensive flickering delicacy, running up his shirt until he slapped it off and ground its existence out under a heel, irrelevantly absorbed in killing it, taking as long as he could to kill it, because after that they had to talk.

When she's done crying, he rubs her back for her, its scarps and indentations, its female lack of complexity and its fever-heat all appealing, but when he cups her breast she says "Just don't touch me" from the very brink of sleep. He says "No?" and she says "No." She's asleep.

He leans in Cindy's doorway, black-leather jacket and dumb, really out-of-the-blue hurt: *No.* Cindy rests on her side, watching TV with one eye closed, the eye against the pillow. The other eye takes him in and returns to the TV, and he asks her, "Does Mommy have a new friend?"

Here's the crazy ready honesty of love: "She has Jeff."

"Who's Jeff, sweetie?"

She sits up, and he takes a Kleenex from the box on her bureau and swipes under her nose. She says, "There's more snot," and he swipes again, sitting down on her bed.

"You've never said 'snot' before."

"You're not here. I say 'shit' too."

"Sometimes I'm here. I'm here now, and you can't say 'snot' or 'shit,' O.K.?"

"This isn't one of your days," she says critically.

"I think we need more days."

"Daddy, you're a horse."

"A horse?"

She says, "Horses stand up when they watch TV."

Obediently he stands, back to her wall, and tells Cindy, "I never in a million years thought you'd be so beautiful."

She says with satisfaction, "But I am."

"Who is Jeff?"

"I'm not supposed to tell you who he is."

"Do we keep secrets?"

"Jeff my teacher."

"Oh, right, Jeff your teacher." Silence except for the TV. "Is he nice?"

"You *are* nice or you can't be a teacher."

James says, "Right. So really nice? Or regular nice?"

"He has no bottom teeth in front."

"Is he nice except for that?"

"When you look at him you just want him to have teeth."

They watch a half an hour's cartoons—James, to begin with, trying to steady himself by intermittent hits of his flushed daughter's beauty. From Acme Trap Co., the coyote orders increasingly fantastic contraptions. Hope is like that, it loves winging it. A trap goes off in bells, explosions, billowing dust, Wile E. Coyote ecstatic but—*neep neep.* Cindy is, before he's entirely all right with this development, dreaming. He wipes as tenderly as possible under her runny nose, then collects her from the bed, her arms and legs ungainly with deep sleep. He cradles her against his chest, swinging her artfully as he walks to ensure her sleep, but she wakes, as he's latching her seat belt, enough to ask, "Does Mommy know I'm leaving?" "She's sleeping. You and I are going for a ride." "Why?" "I wanted a little more time with you." "Why?" "I couldn't go out that door without you." "Why?" "Because I should have been able to but I wasn't, because you were so beautiful and I felt like I was leaving you so far behind me, like you were getting smaller and smaller on the horizon, when all I wanted was to be right back with you and be your dad."

"What's the horizon?"

"I drive, all right? And you sleep, all right?"

James loved sleeping while his father drove. He drove so tirelessly—his expertise matching, for once, what he was doing, the pitch of his concentration confined to what was actually before him, none of that dangerous excess, that spillover James associated with his father—that James could sleep with a clear conscience, temporarily relieved of the burden of his father, leaving his father to himself, adult, awake, fine. James could sleep because his father was fine. On certain long drives James experienced himself, as he was to have few occasions for experiencing himself, as the child, his father's child, and secure. Now let Cindy be the child, be, with surpassing security, his kid, James's baby, in whose presence he can do no wrong. He's pleased with her for the kidlike grace with which she's found a way to sleep in her corner. Because her face is turned from him, all he can see is the rise of her cheek and the modeling of her brow and the corner of her closed eye, and her

ear with the tiny hole in its lobe. He's repeatedly struck by
that minute hole. He didn't know her ears were pierced, and
it summons up for him all that he's not going to know about
her, the wilderness of her private life, the problem of her
existing beyond his ken, his ignorance and bewilderment crim-
inal, his love for her capable of blazing up to shock him.

By the time Cindy wakes it's nearly dark, and the distance
has been covered aimlessly enough to make her wonder what's
going on. All five-year-olds, maybe, love purpose, and are
trying to take their bearings from adults hardly confident of
their own motives: if the extent of everybody's uncertainty
about everything were ever revealed, the blow would be crush-
ing. She says, "Are we going to Granna and Grandpa's?"—
Theresa's mother and father, who live in southern Colorado,
and James is interested that Cindy got the direction right.
Luck, or does she recognize the road? James tells her no. She
says, "Are we going nowhere, then?"

"A kind of nowhere, uh-huh, except it's an all-right nowhere, because you're with me, and I'm with you."

"Why would we go nowhere?"

"I need to think," he tells her. Not an explanation that
can suffice for long, but she absorbs it gravely, and he says
"Look at that" of the big moon rising facing them, the road
arrowing through the desert right to where the moon lofts
upward, and she says, "Daddy, can we get closer to take a
good look?"

He pulls over to the shoulder of the road, and the desert
bleaches out in a wide arc as he swings the truck around, back
the way they came. He lets the truck idle. She unlatches her
seat belt; he leans across to brace her door open so that she can
jump out; she's scared at being by herself *out there;* he thinks
the moonlight raining down should reassure her, but it doesn't;
she finds the stone she wants; she's back beside him in their

small house of the pickup cab, nursing her own daring, curious about its extent and promise, and he doesn't interfere or praise her. So easy to appropriate children's emotions, and disorientingly hard to let them think for themselves about themselves. She stays awake on the trip home, sweet, necessary company.

He doesn't want to deal with Theresa, who's beside the truck before he's turned off the engine, her arms crossed, her teeth chattering. Theresa says, "Fuck, are you trying to kill me from fear?" He says, "It was just a drive," which wasn't what he meant to tell Theresa at all—no, he'd have liked telling her everything, he'd have liked preventing this, her covering her mouth, in fact wedging the back of her hand into her mouth and biting down, and the tears course steadily past the wings of her nose. She rouses herself to cross to the passenger side and take Cindy in her arms. Even as she closes her arms around Cindy she's trying to reason with herself, but this only leaves her high, furious and vivid and well beyond reason, and she strokes her daughter's hair and says, with the peculiar brisk note of parents who are losing it but still confronting a child's needs, "Are you all right? Are you hungry? Did Daddy scare you?"

"We saw the moon and stars and a rabbit ran across the road. We went nowhere."

"Did you wonder what Daddy was *doing?* Are you all right? Are you all right?"

James says, "She's all right."

"I want to sleep in my bed, not in the truck anymore," Cindy says from Theresa's arms to James, and James says, "Why don't you carry her in to bed? Then you and I can talk."

"*Talk,*" Theresa says, and spits at him. He wipes her spit from the corner of his mouth, but it's like a taste, a taint, that got into his mouth, and he's so innocent and injured that he can only get back into his truck and get out of there before she's closed the front door behind her.

This is his town in the evening, streetlights running

through their amber-red-green spectrum over empty intersec-
tions, stars visible even downtown. He can't stop himself.
Some kind of high, grand, last scene is necessary, or this day
will have taught him nothing, he'll never know what moved
him to carry the gun to begin with, and he can't bear that—
can't live with that; can't go home yet. Felipe gives him a
grave smile, holding James by the shoulders to keep him from
the half-empty restaurant. James shrugs him off. "This is one
of your bad ideas," Felipe says.

"You can't say that. You don't know me."

"Are you so hard to know, man?"

Felipe follows him. James rounds on him to get Felipe to
take a few steps backward, and couples at tables glance up,
but can't place the aggression. Hostility's so easily dismissed
in social situations: terrifying to acknowledge, and the long
dining room has a sheltering dimness, so they can't be seen
clearly, and the people are mostly quiet, and James remembers
how tired he is, and thinks he could sit down at a table, and
maybe Felipe would call for Gwen, and Gwen would relent
and get him something to eat—just, however briefly, take
care of him, is there any way on earth to ask for that? What
if those about to embark on the most brutal acts wished only
that? James is neither brutal nor about to be, but his circumstances confuse him, and he wishes that the gun wasn't all
willingness to the hand that holds it.

In the kitchen, the new guy—it has to be the new guy—
sits on a stool meditating over bright-green, bright-red slivers
in a wok while two girls James recognizes chop more vegeta-
bles. They stop this when they see James. Gwen comes out of
the pantry carrying several bottles of wine. She says—not
wanting the new guy to realize she's angry, probably—"Hi."

James says, "Hi. Can we take a minute?"

"James, I'm really tired. It's not a good time for me."

She works at a wine cork while the new guy sticks his hand

out at James. "I'm Evan." James takes his hand and they shake
cleanly, without apprehension. The new guy's too new to know
anything about James; he's caught on enough, though, to want
to know what James will do next. The mood of the kitchen is
of everyone's having worked well together through a long
evening, the end in sight. He's interrupted this, and they
don't quite understand how to sort themselves out, given
James's presence, except for Felipe, who is very sorted out,
who is right behind James. James catches Gwen by the shoulder, and if she hadn't submitted instantly, he would have been
forcing her to turn to face him.

"O.K., James, now what?"

Felipe says, "You be real, real careful now—James, you
listening?"

The new guys says, "What's going on?"

Felipe says, "She don't want him here, and here he is," in
soft explanation to the new guy and the two girls, who've
backed into the counter.

Gwen says, "James, really, what next? Because I can't
guess. I'm so tired of having you walk in just because you
can."

He says, "I won't, after tonight."

"Right." She sees he's serious. "Promise."

"I promise I won't, but I want something first."

Gwen shakes her head and sits down on the stool near the
new guy—Why him, why not Felipe? Because Felipe would
really act?—but James catches her by the wrist and draws her
to her feet and backs Gwen up against the counter by the two
girls, James saying as softly as he can manage, "Hey, Felipe,
man, hold on a minute, hold on," to stave off what Felipe's
dying to do. James swipes a dish towel from the counter and
tells Gwen, "Tie this over my eyes," and turns around; the
towel's dishwater-scented dankness is pleasing, for some obscure reason, and she ties a skillful knot, taking him at his

word, another graceful thing about Gwen. She says, "This is what you want? Always proving something, James. Always."

"You get next to those girls and make it so I don't know who's who, all right? Just do this last favor, all right?"

He listens while they stir themselves into a different lineup against the counter, and then, dazzled by what she's letting him do and blind, he searches the face of the first girl. Her mouth parts at his touch. Even teeth, girl's breath. She wants to say something, but she remembers that her voice would give her away. The pulse at her throat is rapid.

The new guy says, "Why should they do this?"

James skates a hand along the counter until he comes to the naked wrist of the next girl. Under the snug dish towel, he closes his eyes; he searches her face with close, rapid touches and dismisses her. He moves along the counter until his hand meets the hand of the third woman, and that's enough, plenty, conviction. The length of the fingers and the startlingly muscled arm his hand follows to the shoulder is Gwen. He can't be wrong, but he can't not touch her face, either. He says, "It's you," and strokes her lower lip and rests the ball of his thumb on her front teeth, and he keeps thinking her arms will go around him, but they don't. They breathe together like lovers, their mouths only a little distance apart, and he says, "This is you," and it occurs to him he could be wrong, he could be very wrong, but his thumb finds the tiny crescent of scar at the corner of her eye and he says, "I did this to you," and Gwen in his arms doesn't shrug him off or resist him by tensing or do anything but will him away. She wins.

Felipe says, "Enough for tonight now, man. You need to go home, James. She really bears with you, man, but even you know it's over."

"I'm going," James says. "Unless she says not to."

She doesn't say not to, and he unwinds the blindfold and lets it fall. He'd like to say, "This is your last chance," but he can't carry it off, and not saying it is instantly a relief, the right thing, and he shies past Felipe in the doorway and going through the restaurant gets a series of looks he will, for some reason, remember, though they are nobody to him, the people who are looking. He's down the stairs and back into the street, into the *rain*. He is wildly and profoundly amazed at his luck. He will never quite achieve this pitch of strangeness again. His life will go one way, and not the other, and he will find it impossible to say why. He can live with what happens next—he's not going to force it, or himself, ever again, at least not this desperately. He turns into an alley. It's not filthy—Santa Fe alleys never are anymore—but there's a shoddy ruin of a dumpster with rain running down its sides. He goes closer, smelling rank organic rot, and understands it's the restaurant's dumpster, and drops the gun in, down into the cloying rotting dark, which absorbs it with a thud and a rattling-around of cans and a faint chinking of breaking glass. When he gets out of the alley, the rain seems to come from some higher, more ethereal region. It's such sweet rain he turns his face up into. Stunned, enchanted, but very clearheaded, he thinks *Nobody knows. Nobody knows.* He shakes his head. Rain flicks from his hair. He rejoices: *Nobody got hurt.* He feels as if he saved them all.

A Note About the Author

Elizabeth Tallent lives in Little River, California, and in Davis, where she teaches at the University of California. She is the author of two previous collections of stories, *Time with Children* and *In Constant Flight*, and a novel, *Museum Pieces*. Her work has appeared in *The New Yorker*, *Esquire*, *The O. Henry Awards*, *The Best American Short Stories*, *Grand Street*, and *The Paris Review*.

A Note on the Type

The text of this book was set in Garamond, a modern rendering of the type first cut by Claude Garamond (c. 1480–1561). Garamond was a pupil of Geoffroy Tory and is believed to have based his letters on the Venetian models, although he introduced a number of important differences, and it is to him we owe the letter which we know as "old style." He gave to his letters a certain elegance and a feeling of movement that won for their creator an immediate reputation and the patronage of Francis I of France.

Composed by Crane Typesetting Service, Inc.,
West Barnstable, Massachusetts

Printed and bound by Arcata Graphics/Martinsburg,
Martinsburg, West Virginia

Designed by Dorothy S. Baker